The
Pumpkin
Patch

Bed and Breakfast

The Pumpkin Patch

Bed and Breakfast

Barbara A. Brandvold

Kravitz and Sons LLC
204 E Arlington Blvd. Suite B
Greenville, NC 27858

Published by Kravitz and Sons LLC.

ISBN: 979-8-89639-516-4 (sc)
ISBN: 979-8-89639-517-1 (e)

Library of Congress Control Number: 2025919214

To my husband, Allan, and to my son, Ricky.
Thank you for your support.

Table Of Contents

A soft ray of sunshine slowly peeked through the slanted blinds in Maude and Dickie's bedroom.

It began to dance across Dickie's face as he lay there staring at the clock. It was five o'clock. He had tossed and turned all night. Time was running out! He had to find a secret recipe and once again be crowned the world's number one pastry chef. He had been living a life of leisure until cooking shows exploded across the television screen. Now, he would have to fight for his title and prove that he was number one. He would have to prove again, that he was the king of the Pastry Chefs.

His parents had mortgaged everything they owned to send him to the best pastry schools. He had studied in Paris, Portugal, San Francisco, New York, Houston, Seattle, Vancouver and even Nashville, Tennessee. But, the school he loved the most was Napa Valley. His parents had given him strength when he was down and pushed him to continue and finally he had become the greatest. He was the greatest! How could this happen? Over and over again he had to prove himself. Well! He wasn't going to let his parents down. He would once again be "The King of the Pastry Chefs" and win the coveted Golden Spatula Award.

He turned his head toward Maude and stared at the back of her head. How could she sleep when he was in such despair? She was his soul mate. He shook her shoulder.

"Maude…Maude! Wake up! You've got to get on the computer and find me a winning recipe!"

Maude opened her eyes, rolled over and looked at the clock and then at Dickie. "Go back to sleep, it's early," Maude said as she rolled over and shut her eyes.

"Maude, I can't sleep. I've been awake all night," Dickie complained. He shook Maude's shoulder again. "Wake up!" he demanded.

"Leave me alone," Maude said as she covered her head with the sheet.

"Maude, you don't understand. Pastry chefs are coming out of the woodwork. They're trying to take my title. Maude!" Dickie shouted.

"Leave me alone. You know I'm not a morning person and if you keep this up, you're going to be dead meat. Got it?"

"Okay, best buddy," Dickie said. "Go ahead and sleep while my world crumbles around me. You, who enjoys the delights of my culinary greatness, go ahead and sleep." Dickie got up and walked toward the kitchen.

"Dickie! You are soooooo melodramatic! You should get an award for acting," Maude was shouting to him with her head still under the covers.

Dickie walked into the kitchen and stopped in front of the calendar. He stood there staring at it for a long time until he realized there was something written on October 31, Halloween night. That was the night of their anniversary; that was when he had won his first baking contest. What a way to celebrate. Marry your soul buddy and the world will be yours. Yes! That's what he thought and now, he was under attack from all these chefs that came out of nowhere. What was he going to do? He could sneak in and put plastic explosives in their yeast. No! That wouldn't work. If he was the only one that succeeded, then they would know he did it. What else could he think of? There had to be an answer.

Dickie took the calendar off the wall and walked back to the bedroom. "Maude! We can't be going on any trips until I come up with a winning recipe!"

"Dickie! I told you to leave me alone," Maude said as she ripped the cover back and stared into Dickie's eyes. "Since when do you read calendars? Why now?"

Maude climbed out of bed and walked into the bathroom and slammed the door. Dickie scratched his head. "Gee! You don't have to get so mad at me. I only wanted to know what THE PUMPKIN PATCH is."

He could hear her brushing her teeth and then gargle her throat. Dickie sat down on the bed and waited for her to come out. Maude opened the door. "Oh! You're still here?" she said as she walked toward the closet.

"Well, yeah! I live here! Maude? What did I say?" Dickie asked.

Maude stopped and turned around and looked at Dickie. "You blew it. That's what you did. When do you ever look at the calendar? THE PUMPKIN PATCH was my surprise to you for our anniversary. They make the world's best pumpkin bread. It's to die for. But, no! You had to read the calendar. We were going to go and steal the recipe and then you would be king!"

Dickie smiled as he looked at Maude. "But Maude! You've never done anything like that in your life."

"I suppose you haven't thought of putting explosives in your competition's yeast?" Maude asked. Dickie turned around to look at her.

"How could you think I would do something like that? That would be cheating," Dickie said as he turned to face the window. She was reading his mind again.

"Besides, the lady that answered the phone said they had millions of pumpkins. Who would miss one little pumpkin? If she's as old as she sounds, it shouldn't be a problem. When they go to sleep, we'll sneak into the kitchen and find the recipe and take a pumpkin on the way out."

"How did you find out about this place?" Dickie asked her.

"My sister told me about it. She raved about it and she said she desperately wanted to help you win," Maude said as she picked up her brush from the dresser and brushed her hair.

"Your sister! She hates us! She's probably hoping that all the pumpkins will eat us," Dickie cried.

"There you go again, being so melodramatic. If the pumpkin cookies and bread are anything like my sister says they are, you'll have your winning recipe."

"I knew I could count on you. I just can't believe your sister wanted to help me. Why would she want me to continue to be king? Anyway, I just really want to win this award for my parents. It's sort of a thank you for all they did for me."

Dickie walked over to Maude and gave her a great big kiss. "When do we leave?"

"I have it all set up for Saturday, October 31st. The lady at the inn was really nice. She asked me a strange question though."

"What was that?" Dickie asked.

"She asked me if we would be bringing a cell phone? I thought that was really interesting."

"What did you tell her since our cell phones aren't working?" Dickie asked with curiosity.

"Well! As a matter of fact, my sister suggested that we take her phone in case of emergency. So, I said we would. You know, with the new car and all."

"This is getting really weird. Your sister hasn't been this nice to us in years. Oh, well! I guess she's right. Driving up the coast in our new little red sports car should be a lot of fun. Don't you agree?

"Yes, Dickie! I'm really looking forward to it. The lady on the phone said they had spectacular views and millions of pumpkins and its right above the ocean. Won't it be great? You get your recipe and we get a wonderful weekend for our anniversary."

"How long have you known about this?" Dickie asked with a great big grin on his face.

"Since the night you came home and fell asleep on the sofa," Maude replied as she put her arms around him and kissed him. "You were so cute. You still had your uniform on and your great big chef's hat. You fell asleep and the hat just sat there like it was on its throne."

"I checked it out on the Internet and the bed and breakfast got high ratings. The food critics haven't turned in a response but maybe that's because it's new. No! That can't be right. The lady that answered the phone said they had been there forever. Hmmm! What harm could a little old lady do? They had better watch out for us, the King of the Pastry Chefs and his queen!"

2

"I can't believe the past couple of weeks have blown by so fast," Dickie said as he put their luggage on the luggage carrier of his new little red roadster convertible. "The weather is perfect for driving up the coast with the top down."

"It should be a wonderful drive up the coast. I've never known it to be so warm this time of year, have you?"

"No! But it will be great for the pumpkins." Dickie laughed.

Maude laughed and went back into the house to check everything one more time. She checked all the doors and windows and made sure her plants had plenty of water. Normally she wouldn't worry. But, because it was so warm and because they were going to be gone a few days, she wanted to make sure the plants were wet.

Maude walked into the bedroom and picked up George, her favorite stuffed bear and brought him into the living room. George had been with her since she was a child. He was always there when she needed someone to talk to. His long nose was smashed in and that was the way she felt a lot of times when she came home from work. Just looking at him made her laugh. She gave him a big hug and then sat him down on the chair facing the door.

"Okay, George, you're in charge. Make sure you take care of our house and all of Dickie's awards." She was ready. Maude walked outside and locked the front door. She walked to the car to find Dickie sitting behind the wheel ready to go.

"Do you have the directions?" Dickie asked Maude. Maude got in the car and reached in her bag and pulled out the directions that she had received from The Pumpkin Patch.

"Let's see where we're going…If we go up the coast on Highway 101, we will run right into the Seventeen Mile Drive," Maude said as she looked at the map.

"The Bed and Breakfast is on Seventeen Mile Drive? Are you sure? I thought all those homes were residential."

"Yes! That's what she said. It sounds wonderful. Agnes said we would have panoramic views of the ocean and all the pumpkins. They've owned the property for years so maybe that's why they're on Seventeen Mile Drive."

"Who's Agnes?" Dickie asked.

"Agnes is the lady at the Bed and Breakfast. She sounds like a wonderful little old lady," Maude exclaimed.

"I still can't believe that we could get a reservation this time of the year," Dickie said as he put his sunglasses on.

"My sister told me to mention her name and that we would get a room and it worked," Maude said with a big smile.

"Oh, here we go again. Let's not talk about her. I get cold chills just thinking of her. By the way, what happened in court yesterday? Did she inherit all the money from her late husband?"

"Yes! The seven years was up last month and her attorney handled everything for her. It's really sad that he just up and disappeared."

"Yeah! Well, if I was married to her I think I would up and disappear too," Dickie said jokingly.

"Oh, she's not that bad. She's just a little self-centered."

"Yeah, you got that right. Remember the time we threw a big party after I won my first Chef's Hat?"

"Yeah!" Maude replied as she continued to look at the map. "And what did she do? She arrived late as usual. She had to trip down the steps and get everyone to revel around her and forget all about me and my award. How many times has she walked down those stairs? She had to have everyone sit and hold her hand until the ambulance arrived and then she had to come back in her stinky little cast at midnight and make everybody feel sorry for her. Do you remember that?

"Yes! I will admit that she is really insecure. But! I look at it in another way. She had to wear that stinky little cast for three months. That's what I think is funny. In order to hurt you, she hurt herself. I think that's just downright stupid. But some people are like that. But what she doesn't realize is that we partied on without her. Anyway, I'm happy for her. Now, she has millions and loads of real estate and she won't have time to think about us. She'll be worried about where to go shopping next."

"But the time that really gets me is the time that you won the coveted Cookie Cutter Award. Remember? We have just moved into our new house and we threw a really big party to celebrate your award and our new house. Remember?"

Dickie had a funny look on his face. "You forgot?" Maude was surprised.

"Everyone was there except my sister. We were having a great time and all the kids were in the pool and my sister arrived late as usual. When she came in, I mentioned to you that it looked like she had been crying. Remember?"

"No! Sorry!" Dickie replied.

"You only remember when it applies to you? Is that it?" Maude laughed.

"No. I just can't remember: refresh my memory," Dickie said. "The weather was perfect. It was eighty degrees. A slight ocean breeze was blowing. The kids were in the pool. You were still floating on cloud nine because you had won the Golden Cookie Cutter Award. Every time you had a Corona, you tapped your award and said. "Here's to the king!" I was sitting on the patio having a great time laughing and talking to my friends and the next thing I know is my mother is standing in front of me yelling at me, pointing her finger at my nose and I have no idea what she is saying because I was sitting in front of the speaker and the music was loud and all I could do is look at her and watch her mouth going a mile a minute. Then, she turned and stomped out the door."

"Oh, yeah! It's slowly coming back to me! She didn't even look at our new house. She just walked over to the bar, got a drink, drank it and then proceeded to chew you out. But! Before she stomped out the door she walked over and hugged your sister and your mom patted her on the back and they both turned around and looked at you and then she stomped out the door."

"Yes. That's the time. I still for the life of me can't figure out what my mom said and I asked her about it and she said it's over and forget it. I just have this awful feeling my sister told her a bunch of lies and she took it out on me as usual."

"I think that was the night I decided to get real drunk. How many margaritas did I drink?"

"I don't know cause you started making them yourself. That's when it got real scary. I really wanted you that night but all you wanted was your tequila bottle. You even fell asleep hugging the bottle, didn't you?" Dickie was laughing.

"If I remember correctly, you gave me that bottle for my breakfast the next morning, didn't you?" Maude was now laughing.

"Well, I wanted to give you something original and different. I just didn't expect you to run to the bathroom and throw up at the sight of it, though."

"I didn't expect that either," said Maude. "That happened to me a long time ago on a Caribbean Cruise. My girlfriend and I had a drinking contest and of course I lost. I drank too many Yellowbirds and I couldn't drink orange juice for years without getting nauseated." Maude winced at the thought.

"Anyway, are we going through Malibu?" Maude asked.

"Yes. We haven't been through there in years and I'd like to see how it has changed, don't you?"

"Let's get going, it's hot sitting here in the sun," Maude said as Dickie turned the ignition on and the little roadster's engine purred.

"Just listen to that, what a car!" Dickie said as he pressed on the gas pedal and the little shiny, red roadster sped down the street toward the freeway. Maude loved to ride in the roadster with the top down, sitting next to Dickie, the love of her life.

Maude and Dickie had first met in kindergarten. Yes, kindergarten. It was love at first sight for Maude. She had not wanted to go to school. She would have preferred to stay at home with her mother. But, her mother had other ideas. Maude's baby sister had been born and her mother spent most of her time tending to her every need.

She was practically dragged into the classroom. She was crying and pleading with her mom to let her go home. Dickie saw Maude crying and walked over and put his arm around her and said, "I'll take care of you. Don't worry. Everything will be fine."

Maude looked in his eyes and knew she had found a friend for life; he was someone she could trust. She quickly wiped away her tears and took his hand and walked behind him over to the floor where all the children were sitting and sat down next to him. They looked at each other and knew they would be friends for life. She never looked back at her mother.

3

Maude and Dickie stopped at the Big Rock Restaurant for lunch. The restaurant is cantilevered out over the ocean with only two beams holding it in place; if you're afraid of heights, this is not the place to stop and eat. However, Maude and Dickie loved this restaurant because it was at the very end of the Malibu strip. They were seated at a table at the edge of the balcony that overlooked the ocean. Normally, sitting at this table would guarantee you getting a free bath from the surf pounding the rocks. The spray would shoot high up into the air, over the glass partition. But today, the sea was calm. This was their favorite spot to eat fresh fish. What else could you ask for on a beautiful day like this in sunny Southern California?

Maude gazed at the ocean in search of dolphins. She watched the seagulls dip into the ocean for fish. She watched in awe as a huge pelican slowly floated by and landed in the tranquil sea. The water was so smooth; it was just like a piece of glass. It was almost eerie!

"Dickie! Have you noticed how calm the ocean is today?" Maude asked.

"No! I'm busy trying to decide what I'm going to eat. Everything sounds so good." Dickie continued to read the menu.

"Well! I'm going to order the same old thing I always order," Maude replied as she continued to gaze at the ocean.

Just as the waiter walked up to the table, Maude jumped out of her chair. The waiter spilled the water all over the table.

"Oh, my gosh! I'm so sorry," he said.

"Don't worry, it was my fault," Maude replied as she brushed herself off.

"Why did you jump up like that?" Dickie asked.

"I saw a school of dolphins playing in the water and I wanted to show you," Maude said excitedly.

"I'm so sorry," the waiter replied again.

"Don't worry. My wife gets excited over little things like that. I'm sure she meant you no harm." The waiter headed back to the kitchen.

"You turkey! I meant no harm? Just wait till I get a hold of you tonight. See how much harm comes to you!" Maude was smiling.

"Well! We'll probably have to see if those little old ladies are hard of hearing. But! First, we have to eat." Dickie motioned for the waiter to return.

Maude sat there looking at the calm ocean as Dickie ordered for both of them.

After the waiter left Maude looked at Dickie and said, "Don't you find it a little odd that today the ocean is calm and there's going to be a big, full moon tonight."

"No! Weather patterns change from year to year. Maybe! Just maybe! This weather is happening just for us."

Maude looked at Dickie with a blank look on her face.

"You know. A full moon brings a lot of light. What is it they say? By the light of the full moon, your dreams can come true. All I need is just enough light to steal one itty, bitty, perfect pumpkin and we'll be in business." Dickie looked out toward the ocean.

"No! I think it's by the light of the full moon that werewolves start to prowl…our only hope is that one of the little old ladies isn't a werewolf and we'll be in business!"

"You and your animals," Dickie said as the waiter returned with their food.

"Wow! That was really fast!"

"Oh, wow! This looks wonderful," Maude told the waiter.

The waiter asked Maude if she would like anything to drink and before she could respond, Dickie said, "I think we had better keep the water away from her."

"Yes, I would like another glass of water, please," Maude replied.

The waiter disappeared into the kitchen.

Maude took a bite of her salad and savored the taste and then she looked out toward the ocean and sat there listening.

"Maude, what are you doing?" Dickie asked.

"I'm listening," She replied.

"I know that. But what are you listening to?" Dickie asked.

"That's just it, I'm not listening to anything," she responded with a serious look on her face as she turned to look at the ocean again.

"Dickie! Something is wrong, seriously wrong."

"What are you talking about?" he demanded.

"There are no sounds. Listen! There are no sounds."

"How can I listen if you keep talking?" Dickie quipped.

Maude took another bite of her shrimp and let it slowly dissolve in her mouth. She listened again as she stared at the ocean. The seagulls floated by without a sound. Normally, you can't hear yourself think. The ocean was very smooth. The dolphins had disappeared; the pelican had also disappeared.

The waiter returned and put their bill on the table. He then turned around, took off his apron, hung it on the rack and headed out the door. Two other waiters left with him.

"Dickie look, the waiters are leaving! Something is going on." Maude cried.

"You must find out what's happening."

"Okay! Okay! I can't finish my lunch with you going crazy," Dickie said as he got up, threw his napkin in his chair and walked over to the cashier.

"I know this sounds crazy. My wife is going nuts. Why are all the waiters leaving?"

The cashier looked at Dickie and then looked at Maude who was sitting there staring at both of them.

"They're leaving because their shift is over," she responded. The cashier turned and walked away.

Dickie turned purple and walked back to the table.

"What happened? Your face is bright red," Maude said.

"Well! It should be," Dickie said as he sat down.

"So? Where did they all go and shouldn't we be leaving too?" Maude practically screamed.

"Geez! Calm down," Dickie said under his breath. "They left because their shift is over."

Maude stared at Dickie. She sat up straight. "Well! That doesn't explain why everything is so quiet."

"Geez! Give it a break! Can I finish my lunch in peace and quiet?" Dickie stabbed at his salad and worried that he had said the wrong thing. He didn't look up at Maude.

Maude took a bite and then looked out the window. She slowly finished her lunch and watched for some sign. She noticed that the palm trees weren't swaying either. She started to tell Dickie, but then she knew he would just make fun of her. She sat there and watched and waited for them to move.

"Are you through eating?" Dickie asked. Maude nodded her head.

Dickie picked the bill up from the table and walked over to the cashier. He paid the bill as Maude walked past him to the outside. Dickie walked up to Maude and put his arm around her and pulled her close.

"Don't ruin our trip by worrying too much," Dickie said as he nuzzled her neck.

"Dickie! I know what it is," Maude said as she turned to look at Dickie. "We're going to have an earthquake. That's it. I know it."

"How do you know that?" Dickie said poking fun at her.

"Because! The weather gets really weird and quiet. Remember the last earthquake? You couldn't hear any of the dogs in the neighborhood. The birds stopped chirping. Remember?" Maude asked.

"The only thing I remember about that earthquake is that I had just won my first Golden Banana Award and we were giving your mother a big birthday party to celebrate her birthday and my award."

Dickie and Maude continued to talk as they got in the car. They put their hats and sunglasses on and got ready to drive up the coast.

"Oh, yeah! I remember that. We're sitting there waiting with our guest and all of a sudden, the next thing we know is that my mom and sister are on their way to Hawaii. They call us from the airplane to say my mom really wanted to go to Hawaii instead of having a party because everyone would know it was her birthday and that she was getting older. We sat there with all the food and all her friends. How did they get reservations so fast? And come to think of it, my sister's husband didn't go along with them either. I hadn't thought of that till right now. Hmm! I was so ticked off at both of them. Strange, isn't it?" Maude sat there wondering what really happened.

"I think the earthquake was probably caused by your coming unglued. I've never seen you so mad. You were shaking violently. But you put it behind you and continued with the party. You're a real trouper when it comes to taking care of me," Dickie said this with pride.

"If it hadn't been so hot, I don't think I would have got so mad. You know how the heat affects me when I drink. But we still had fun. Now that I think of it, we probably had more fun with them not being there. Your golden banana was the talk of the party. I didn't know little old ladies liked dirty jokes as much as they did. I never knew you could do so many things with a banana either."

"Yeah and I'm going to show you tonight that my golden banana is still alive and well," Dickie said with a big grin.

"Promises! Promises!" Maude said as Dickie floored the gas and headed to the coast.

All of a sudden, a big gust of wind came up and blew Dickie's hat off his head and out into the road. Dickie pulled over to the side of the road and started to get out of the car to get his hat but Maude grabbed his arm.

"Look at your hat! It's flying across the road toward the ocean." Maude exclaimed.

Dickie watched as his hat flew up and out into the ocean. "That's my good luck hat. What will I do without it?"

"We'll buy you another one when we get to Santa Barbara," Maude replied.

"You don't understand, a man's hat is like his sword," Dickie cried. "It protects him from all evil!"

"Oh, here we go again. You're being so melodramatic again. A hat is a hat!" Maude was laughing.

"Oh really! Then why do you wear a certain pair of shoes every time you have a big, important meeting with clients?"

Maude looked at Dickie with a smug look on her face. "Because, my dear husband, they match my outfit."

"And why, pray tell, does it take you hours to find that outfit that will match a certain pair of shoes that we're discussing?" Dickie asked with a smirk on his face.

"Okay! Okay! I see that I'm not going to win. We can't do anything about your hat now, unless you feel like swimming, so I suggest that we plan on picking up a new one in Santa Barbara."

"What would The Iron Chef do in a case like this?" Dickie asked himself.

"He would find another good luck symbol and get on with it. Yes! That's what he would do," Dickie decided.

Maude watched and listened with amusement.

"Yes, if my good luck symbol has disappeared, I must find another good luck piece," Dickie said as he continued to talk to himself. "Dickie! Did you wear that hat under your chef's hat? Maude asked.

"Yes! All the time and now I've lost my power and good luck and you're interrupting my train of thought," Dickie replied.

"Oh, excuse me! Maybe I should call Bobby Flay and see what he would do in a situation like this."

Dickie turned toward Maude and just glared at her. He looked back to see if any traffic was approaching and eased the car out onto the road and pressed on the gas. He looked out toward the ocean once more. His good luck hat had disappeared, he was on his own.

Maude sat there quietly for a minute. "Did you bring my favorite CD?"

Dickie pushed the button without responding. Music filled the air.

Maude loved the Statler Brothers. She began singing along with the CD.

"Have you ever passed the corner
Of 4th and Grand
Where a little ball of rhythm's
Got a shoeshine stand
He's a great big bundle of joy."

"Come on, Dickie, please sing with me." Dickie looked at Maude with a frustrated look on his face.

He then reached over, pushed the button, started the CD again and then began singing the words with her together with the Statler Brothers.

"Just because I asked a friend about her
Just because I spoke her name somewhere
Just because I rang her number
By mistake today
She thinks I still care."

They exited the freeway at Cabrillo Boulevard and for the moment, Dickie seemed to forget about his favorite hat.

4

Dickie and Maude drove up the main street. At first, they saw people lined up on the grassy areas with their paintings scattered everywhere. Beyond the crowds they saw the white, sandy beach that stretches out to the Pacific Ocean. The beach was crowded with people because it was the weekend and a warm breeze was floating through the air. Dickie turned the music down and listened to the hustle and bustle of the people walking along the sidewalks and stopping to look at the paintings.

"Santa Barbara is one of the most beautiful cities in the world," Maude said. "It sure comes alive during the summer. Don't you agree?"

"Only if it has a hat store!" Dickie exclaimed.

"I sure hope so, if not, I'm sure Carmel will have one," Maude said.

"Yes! But we're not going to Carmel until after we go to the bed and breakfast, right?"

"Oh, yeah! Well! Let's see what we can find before we get worried. Besides, I haven't been shopping in a long time."

"A long time, like in a week?"

Maude glared at Dickie. "And what did I have to buy the last time I went shopping? Do you, almighty one, remember what I was sent to search for and find?"

"There you go again. Why do I always get the blame for your shopping trips?"

"Because, I don't need new aprons, I don't cook, your highness!" Maude teased.

"I think I need a cocktail. I have a brilliant idea. Let's check into our hotel and then find an outside café that will serve cocktails and let's order one of those new little drinks that Sandra Lee made on her show."

"Only if you promise me that you won't be thinking about her gorgeous eyes while you're drinking your drink," Maude replied.

"Now, Maude! You can rest assured that I won't be thinking about her eyes. When have I ever given you cause to doubt my love for you?"

"You know I have to keep up on all my competition, no matter whether it's male or female."

"All I gotta say is those two cute little guys on the Road Trip sure keeps my engine going," Maude said laughing.

"Yeah! You better watch out cause their momma will sure have your hide if you think about them too often, especially since one of them just got married. She might just put you in one of her baking dishes and forget to turn off the oven."

"Naw, I just saw her on Oprah, so she's busy, and I'm sure she's got things to do with her busy schedule and she won't have time to keep her eyes on her boys," Maude said.

Dickie drove down the street until he found their hotel, the wonderful Hotel Alexander. Maude loved the big blue canopies, the white stucco buildings with wonderful terra cotta tiles on the roof and the fact that it was right across the street from the ocean. They always stay at this hotel because it is a couple of blocks from the pier. When they get ready for dinner, they can walk down to the restaurant on the pier instead of having to drive. Their employees always have a good attitude. Dickie pulled into the parking lot and found a safe parking spot for his new little toy. He got out and stretched and then untied their suitcase from the rack on the back of their car and then they walked into the hotel lobby.

Dickie and Maude walked up to the counter. A young girl was working the desk. She stood with her back to them and when she turned around to face them it was all Maude could do not to gasp at the image the girl portrayed. She reminded Maude of how she looked twenty years ago. The first thing that you noticed was the girl's long, beautiful auburn hair. It was the most beautiful color of copper that she had seen in years and as shiny as the hair of a beautiful stallion. Then, when she looked at you, you couldn't take your eyes off her gorgeous deep blue eyes with the thick long lashes. When she smiled at them, Maude just stood there. Where had time gone? The twenty years was gone and she would never get it back but she had done her best to keep herself in great shape. She looked at Dickie and he was as mesmerized as she was. Dickie finally spoke to her.

"We have reservations," Dickie said as he handed her his driver's license. They registered and got the keys to their room and walked silently upstairs to check it out. Dickie unlocked the door and they walked in. Maude surveyed the room with its wonderful shades of pale blue and rattan furniture and immediately went to the window to see the view and get some fresh air. She pulled the curtains back and opened the sliding glass door and walked out onto the patio. She stood there in silence listening to the sound of the ocean. Dickie sat the suitcase down on the bed and walked over to Maude and looked out at the ocean.

"The view is great," Dickie said as he turned to face her. "Maude, about that girl downstairs. I wasn't flirting with her. I could have sworn I had seen her before and that I knew her."

"You don't have to apologize. You did know her! She's me twenty years ago. I couldn't speak because I realized that I used to be her and that time is flying by us really fast. It's too bad she isn't my little sister."

"Yeah! I wouldn't mind having her around at all!" Dickie said jokingly as he looked at Maude. "I'm sorry, I shouldn't have said that."

"It's okay! All I have to say is that I'm a little wiser and a tiny bit older and right now I think I need that cocktail." Maude pulled Dickie into the room and closed the sliding door.

Dickie stopped Maude and put his arms around her and kissed her. "Maude, I wouldn't trade you for anyone in the world, no matter how young or beautiful they look. You and I have grown older together and we're partners for life. Do you remember the first time I say you?"

"Yes! I think about that often!"

"I told you that I would take care of you forever. Well, I meant it and nothing is going to change that. So now, we both need a drink."

They walked down to the main level and out onto the street and walked down the sidewalk. Maude looked across the street at all the people and listened to all the noise they were making. Off in the distance, she could hear some musicians.

"Can you hear the music coming from down the street?" she asked.

"Yes! I think it's reggae," Dickie answered.

"Sounds great to me," Maude said. She stopped in front of a cute little café with a huge courtyard paved with cobblestone and tables set under big, brilliant brick red umbrellas. If you take a deep breath, you can inhale the wonderful, fragrant aroma of the jasmine and the huge red California roses. Dickie and Maude chose a seat close to the sidewalk so they could watch all the activity.

The waiter walked up to them and Dickie asked if they could make a watermelon martini.

"I don't think we've ever made that one," the waiter replied.

"You guys don't watch the cooking channel?" Dickie inquired.

"No sir! We don't have time to do anything but cook," the waiter replied again.

"Not only are you missing great food but the cooks are also wonderful to look at," Dickie said with a chuckle.

"Well, Dickie, I suggest that we just order a plain old Cosmopolitan and maybe they could put a scope of watermelon in it."

"I'll go check it out and come right back," he said as he turned around and walked into the café.

"Isn't this fresh air wonderful?" Maude said as she looked around.

"It won't be wonderful till I find myself a new hat," Dickie replied.

"Does that mean that I only get one drink?" Maude asked.

"Well, if you get two drinks, we'll be going to bed early cause you know how you are with drinks."

"Just because I can't handle alcohol, doesn't mean I don't like to have a good time," Maude complained.

"I know! I know! But, I've got to find a new hat and you're no good if you've had a lot to drink."

The waiter returned with two Cosmos on his tray and set them down in front of them.

"Will this do? The waiter said with a big smile on his face.

"It looks fabulous. So! You had watermelon after all? It tastes wonderful too." The waiter was very pleased with himself, smiling as he walked away.

Dickie picked up his drink and tasted it. "Wow! This is good. Here's to Sandra Lee and her wonderful concoctions"

"And?" Maude signed.

"Oh, yes! Here's to Sandra Lee's big beautiful eyes."

"No, I didn't mean that," Maude said.

"And to my wonderful, beautiful wife," Dickie said as he took another sip of his drink.

"And?" Maude continued to question.

"And, what? What could I have missed? My every thought is about you except when I have to watch my competition to make sure that I keep the upper hand."

The waiter came back. "I just wanted to see if your drink was still okay."

"Oh, yes!" Maude said.'

"Would you like another one?" he asked.

"No! We have to go shopping first and then we'll come back for another one. Won't we, Dickie?"

"Well, I'll be right here when you get back," said the waiter as he laid their bill down on the table and then walked back into the café.

Dickie looked at the bill and pulled twenty dollars out of his wallet and put it on the table with the check. They finished their drinks and then got up and walked down the street to look for a hat store.

5

A radiant beam of sunshine danced through the windows of the garden room at The Pumpkin Patch Bed and Breakfast.

The house is situated on ten acres of land at the very end of the 17 Mile Drive depending on which way you enter the drive. It sits on a point between Pebble Beach and the Cypress Point Golf Course. According to the Real Estate Magazine for Monterey County, this piece of land is worth more than the whole city put together.

The 5700-square-foot house was built two hundred and twenty-five feet from the edge of the cliff and the Pacific Ocean. The owner commissioned a contractor to build a strong, soundproof house that would protect against the harsh winds that blew in off the ocean during the winter months. He chose to inset one foot of concrete between all the walls and he also chose to apply one foot of stucco to the outside walls. The main studs were upgraded to four by sixes instead of two by fours to hold the weight. The owner chose to have his stucco a creamy white; he thought the sun would beam off his house onto the pumpkin fields and thus help his pumpkins grow faster.

A ten-foot, glass enclosed veranda was built around the entire house so that the owner, at any time, could sit in his rocker and gaze upon his pumpkin fields with pride. The glass was partitioned so that it could be opened during the spring and summer.

Now, every afternoon, you will find Alice and Agnes sitting on the veranda in their favorite chair, watching their special pumpkins. These pumpkins are planted in special, raised beds. They are given special nutrients to make them grow. No one is allowed to touch these pumpkins except Alice and Agnes.

In an effort to protect the special pumpkins, Alice and Agnes have placed their most trusted pumpkin people in front of these beds and they also have their faithful black cats keeping an eye on them.

Inside the house, each bedroom is quite cozy and has a huge picture window so that you can see the pumpkin fields and the Pacific Ocean; these windows can also be opened to let in the fresh ocean breeze. The beds have big, wonderful soft mattresses. After Alice and Agnes took over running the house, they decided to furnish each room with oversized chairs that would give their guests the utmost in comfort. They wanted to make sure their guests were very happy.

The garden room is on the first floor; it is the room where they normally serve breakfast, lunch and dinner. In this room, there is a panoramic view of the pumpkin fields and the ocean. During the spring and summer, they open the windows and at night, you can hear a sound that sounds like little murmurs. In the middle of the room sits a large table big enough to serve ten people but Alice and Agnes never have more than two guests at a time.

When the west wind comes in off the ocean, it sounds like the pumpkins are whistling.

There is a door in the garden room that leads to the cellar, where Alice and Agnes keep all their prized possessions. Normally the door's locked, but today, the door is unlocked, as they are getting ready for their next guest.

Alice is down in the cellar checking to make sure that Agnes has arranged their jars in order so that when she needs one, she can grab it in a hurry. Agnes refuses to wear her glasses a lot of the time and it drives Alice nuts.

The grounds are completely covered with big, beautiful, brilliant orange, scrumptious pumpkins. The weather is perfect for growing pumpkins as it never gets too hot or too cold. A gentle breeze gently floats through the Monterey cypress and crosses over the fields in the month of October creating an unusual sound. Sometimes, people say it sounds as if babies are being lulled to sleep. This is especially true when there is a big, bright full moon.

Alice and Agnes have made sure everything is sparkling clean for their next guest. They are two sisters who have owned the bed and breakfast since their parents' untimely deaths many, many years ago. It wasn't always a bed and breakfast, but Alice and Agnes needed a way to get people to come and visit them, so they decided to change their home to The Pumpkin Patch Bed and Breakfast. Since they are currently the oldest residents of their city, no one objected, especially since their cousin was there to help them out if they needed help.

One wonders how they keep the bed and breakfast so sparkling clean. At their age, people are ready for a rocker, but not these two. Every morning, they are up at the crack of dawn walking every inch of their property.

As you get older, your memory starts to fade, right? Nope! Not these two. At eighty years old, their memory is sharp as a tack! They may look a little disheveled at times, a couple of hairs out of place, a goofy look on their face but that's usually when someone shows up unexpectedly. Agnes sometimes forgets to wear her glasses and Alice gets mad but that's not very often. Agnes gets frustrated and gets things mixed up just because she can't see. But, you bet they know if someone has turned a pumpkin an inch or if there is a new footstep in the garden that wasn't there the day before.

Alice and Agnes had lost some of their pumpkins until they took matters into their own hands and moved the pumpkin people to different areas of their gardens. They have made them look so realistic wearing designed jeans and beautiful designer sweaters and jackets. Their shoes are to die for! The mother pumpkin has jeweled tennis shoes and a gold studded belt that came from Beverly Hills. People driving by usually stop and want to have their picture taken with them.

Alice moved a few of the Pumpkin People closer to the house and put them in their special garden. They keep an eye out for little thieves. The Pumpkin People family has had its share of little kids romping all around them so Alice and Agnes had a huge iron fence and gate installed so no one could enter without them knowing about it.

The baby pumpkin is so cute! She's only four years old and she wears the most gorgeous clothes. Today, she's wearing a yellow Pendleton shirt under her cute little designer coveralls. Alice bought her a wide brim hat with a blue band to match her jeans so that she could keep the crows from landing on her long curly orange hair. When little kids see her, they immediately run over and begin to pull her hair or tickle her nose so Alice had to put a stop to it. She was threatening to put live wires in her coveralls to keep people away but her cousin told her she would get in trouble. The baby is so cute; she is their pride and joy. Alice dreads to see Halloween come because she knows the little monsters will show up.

Alice and Agnes never married because they devoted their whole lives to caring for their parents and the pumpkin fields. Their parents bought this property many, many years ago.

When they were kids they used to sit and listen to all the stories of the people that came to visit. They never questioned their parents as to why the same people didn't come back and visit more than once.

Their mom taught them how to make their special pumpkin bread, and how to make this wonderful, potent tea from the pumpkin seeds. The bread was always warm and full of cinnamon; it seemed as though it had an orange glow to it.

Alice grew weary when her father started giving the pumpkins away. She was afraid they would run out of food and besides, these were their babies. Every time a new person stopped by, he would give them a little pumpkin. They argued every day about this and Alice grew very restless.

One day, she finished counting the pumpkins and she was short by fifty. She immediately ran to her father and told him how many were missing. "Don't worry about those pumpkins. I'm sure someone needed them more than we did," Alice's father replied. "We have thousands."

"But, Papa! These are our babies," Alice cried.

"Child! You act like they're human!" her father said as he continued to hoe the dirt around the pumpkins.

"Oh, you don't understand," Alice said as she ran toward the house. She ran down the steps to hide in the cellar where she could be alone. She sat there for hours in the dark trying to figure out what to do. Suddenly, the door opened and Agnes came flying down the stairs.

"What are you doing down here so long? I'm having to take care of the pumpkins by myself." Agnes said as she sat down next to Alice.

"Papa doesn't understand; he's giving away our babies!" Alice said with tears rolling down her face.

"Well! Maybe we should give Papa away!" Agnes said with a huge smile.

6

Maude and Dickie spent the entire afternoon browsing through the shops looking for a good luck hat for Dickie. He didn't see anything he liked or thought would bring him some good luck. Maude found a hat that she thought was great but Dickie didn't like it. It said, "Give me your dough and I'll make it rise." Dickie thought it was from some bank and didn't have anything to do with cooking dough so she put the hat back on its rack.

It was getting late and they were getting hungry so they decided to walk out to the pier and eat dinner at The Ocean Breeze. They loved this restaurant because you could sit upstairs, have a magnificent view of the harbor, a delicious cocktail and watch for the lights of the city to be turned on and cast a wonderful glow over the water.

The receptionist seated them at a perfect table facing the harbor and most of Cabrillo Boulevard. "I'm hungry! I wonder why I get so hungry when I drink?" Maude said to Dickie as she sat down.

"I don't know cause I eat all the time and I don't drink."

Maude hadn't had time to think about what happened earlier in Malibu. When she remembered it she instantly looked out at the ocean and saw a lot of sea gulls flying vigorously by. She could also hear them squawking at each other so she figured the worst was over, she could relax. Maude could just make out the huge, dark pelicans floating on the water, waiting to catch an unlucky fish coming to the surface for air. The sun was fast descending upon the calm ocean and as they waited for the waiter, Maude began to ask Dickie questions.

"Dickie, have you thought about your recipe at all today? I mean, after you get the pumpkin, what kind of sauce or topping are you going to put on the bread?"

"Shhhh! Somebody might hear you," Dickie said, startled.

"Dickie! No one in here knows about the contest." She looked around the room. "I don't see anyone I recognize. The closest person to us is the guy in Napa and besides it looks like everybody is busy drinking."

Dickie looked around the restaurant and when he felt comfortable he began talking. "Many years ago, my mother used to make this wonderful pumpkin bread with a lot of cinnamon in it. I'll always remember how it smelled as if it was yesterday. I'm going to try and recapture that aroma." The waiter walked up to their table and immediately they stopped talking.

"We'd like to order our drinks and food at the same time if you don't mind," Dickie said to the waiter.

"Certainly! Would you like to have a cocktail or coffee or tea?"

Dickie looked at Maude and as she smiled he spoke to the waiter. "I think we'll both have a Cosmopolitan to drink and then I think we'll both have a seafood salad with honey lemon dressing and then we'll have your wonderful halibut dinner. But! We would like our fish to be cooked well done and not rare."

After the waiter wrote down their order he said, "Got it and I'll be right back with your drinks."

"Now, where were we? I'll know better after I see the pumpkins tomorrow as to how I'll cook them. If they're really ripe, I can't cook them very long and that will depend on how I make my sauce."

"This whole cooking thing is amazing to me. I didn't realize there were so many men that loved to cook. You're lucky your mom taught you how to cook. My mom only taught me how to get lost." The waiter returned with their cocktails and just in time for the beautiful sunset that was slowly cascading over the harbor.

Maude and Dickie toasted each other, took a sip of their drink and stared out the window at the Pacific Ocean.

Maude smiled at Dickie and softly said, "Here's to the King of the Pastry chefs and the king of my heart. May your dough forever rise."

Dickie sat there as tears welled up in his eyes and it was all he could do not to cry. The momentum of the past weeks had caught up with him. He took a sip of his drink and smiled at Maude.

"You are also the queen of my heart and maybe after tomorrow our worries will be over once and for all," Dickie said in a whisper. He added, "I don't like to take advantage of old people but this is considered an emergency. Hopefully those two little old ladies won't mind if I take one of their pumpkins. I can't imagine how they would know how many pumpkins they have. And, I'll also give them an extra big tip just in case they do miss one and to ease my mind of becoming a thief."

Maude smiled at Dickie and said; "I was thinking that after this is over and you're crowned King again and you win the Golden Spatula Award, that you will be able to relax and then, you would meet me in Las Vegas. You know I have to go there for a convention in two weeks and I already have a suite at Caesar's Palace. We could have dinner at Spago's and sit under the stars at the outdoor café. Doesn't that sound good to you?"

Dickie smiled at Maude. He would follow her anywhere. She was the love of his life. So, she was twenty years older-what did that mean? It meant that every time he needed her, she had been there for him. It meant that he loved her more today than he did twenty years ago. She was still beautiful to him. Her copper brown hair was just as fantastic as it was in kindergarten.

Her smile was even brighter and her eyes were still the same, magnificent deep blue that he had fallen in love with in the very beginning.

So she had gained a pound or two; he had also. He looked at Maude.

"You know I was just thinking that when we get home I'd like to turn our extra room into a gym. I can't stop tasting desserts but I have to make an effort to lose this weight that I've gained."

"Now, are you saying that cause of the girl at the hotel or what?"

"Maude, for Pete's sake, I'm saying that cause I don't like to look at myself anymore since I've gained all this weight. My smock is getting very tight."

"But you're a cook and you have to taste your food? Isn't that what cooking's all about?"

"Just think about your idol, Bobby Flay. Is he in good shape or what?"

"Dickie!"

"Don't Dickie me! We're going to do this. I have to do this because I need it for me and if you want me to fly to Vegas and meet you, then you'll have to help me."

"What do you want me to do?"

"Start making me a salad for dinner when I come home instead of pickup food from Harry's. All you have to do is rip a few lettuce leaves apart and stick a few tomatoes in it."

"If it's so easy, why don't you do it?"

"Maude, please! Help me out here. Do you want to help me or what?"

Maude smiled at Dickie and he didn't need an answer.

"Okay, it's settled. When we get home, we'll start with the salads and I'll get the gym up and running."

The waiter arrived with their dinner and set it down in front of them.

"Wow, this looks great," Maude said as she took another sip of her drink.

"Please check your fish to make sure it's cooked enough before I leave," the waiter said.

Dickie cut his fish with his fork and Maude did the same; they were both happy and the waiter walked away.

Maude looked around the room as she ate. The restaurant was very busy, but it usually is this time of year and especially since the weather was still warm. There wasn't an empty table in the room. The décor in the restaurant instantly puts you at ease; most of it is from the fifties and sixties with old pictures of surfers, surfboards and those wonderful woody station wagons covering the walls. The bar was made out of an old, large wooden surfboard polished with a lot of beeswax. The canopies were all from thatched pieces of palm trees leaves.

Somewhere in the background, you could hear the soft sound of Hawaiian music; it just gently floated into the room.

Maude thought it was great that the waiters wore Bermuda shorts; not that they were sexy or anything but just because it fit the theme. She loved their tropical shirts and instantly she had an idea.

"Dickie! I just had a brilliant idea. Let's change our pool into a tropical oasis when we get home."

"Is that before or after we change the extra room into a gym?"

"Why don't you take care of the gym and I'll take care of changing the pool area and I think it's perfect timing. We need to get in shape for all our luaus that we'll be having, so all we'll need now is a suntan room."

Dickie sat there staring at her. When she finally looked up at him she began to laugh.

"Did you think I was serious about the suntan room?"

"Yes as a matter of fact, I did."

"Oh Dickie, I was just pulling your leg but I was serious about changing our décor to a much more relaxed theme where you can sit and have cocktails after a long hard day of eating desserts and by the way, we didn't finish our conversation about your entry in the contest."

"I have it all planned and I think it will work. I'm going to have to try it when we get home but I think it will taste okay."

"Come on, give me the secret. I'm not going to see anybody that counts."

"Okay, but you've got to promise me you won't tell a soul."

Maude smiled and Dickie continued to talk, "I'm going to use canned peaches as an extra ingredient over my pumpkin bread. I'm going to drain them and use the stock to make a succulent paste that

I'll drizzle over the peaches after I've sautéed them in the pan over very low heat. I'll lay the peaches over pumpkin bread and drizzle the paste."

"How are you going to make the paste?"

"I thought I would add a few added ingredients to the stock like cinnamon, nutmeg and a little bit of sugar and one more little secret called honey. I'm going to cook it over very low heat, just until it come to boil and then remove it from the heat and let it set The thing I haven't decided on is whether or not I'll use some chocolate and ginger for a special zing. I think it might be a good idea."

"I should write out my idea so that I don't forget it." Dickie motioned for the waiter to come over.

"Yes, sir, may I help you?"

"Yes! I need to borrow a pencil and a piece of paper if you have it."

The waiter left and returned with a pad and paper for Dickie and then asked if they wanted another cocktail.

Before Dickie could answer Maude had ordered herself another one and suggested that Dickie have one too.

"No! I have work to do tomorrow but you go ahead."

The waiter left and returned shortly with another Cosmopolitan for Maude. She took a sip of the drink as soon as he had set it down.

Dickie hastily wrote down his new secret recipe and sat there staring at it.

3 cups pumpkin (removed from one itty bitty pumpkin and remove seeds
from mix and save)
1 cup sugar
¾ cup plain flour
½ cup whipping cream
2 eggs
1 teaspoon cinnamon
½ cup margarine
½ teaspoon
¾ teaspoon vanilla Preheat oven to 350. Mix all ingredients for pumpkin

bread and bake for 20 minutes.

Sauce for bread: 1 can sliced peaches (open and drain stock into pan)

Bring stock to boil after adding ¾ teaspoon almond extract, 1 dash ginger, 2 tablespoons molasses, 3 tablespoons whipping cream. Stir frequently. Do not let sauce stick or burn.

Heat nonstick skillet over high heat, sauté pumpkin seeds and continue to stir with wooden spoon. Sprinkle sugar over seeds. Lay seeds on flat surface. Melt chocolate in sauce pan.

Dickie stopped writing his new secret recipe because Maude had gotten really quiet. He put the piece of paper in his pocket. As she ate her dinner, she began to smile.

"What're you smiling at?"

"Oh, I was thinking about this dream I had this morning when I woke up. It was really funny."

"Well! Aren't you going to tell me about this dream?"

"Hmmm! I'm not sure you want to hear it but okay." Maude took a big sip of her cocktail and looked down at her plate.

"This morning I dreamed that I was being chased around the golf course by Retief Goosen. I was playing in this golf tournament at work and every time I had to stop my cart, he would come by with this really big smile and say, "I Love you?" Maude laughed.

Dickie wasn't quite sure he heard what she said. "Okay. Let me get this straight. You're dreaming about some guy named, what was it, Retief Goosen?"

"Well, Dickie, it was just a dream! Don't tell me that you don't dream about those girls on the food network channel." Maude took another sip of her drink and continued. "I must have dreamed about him cause they're always giving him a bad time about being so serious. That's why it's so funny…Don't you get it?"

"No!...I just want to know when you have time to watch the golf channel when you're supposed to be watching the food network for me."

"Well, sometimes my hand kinda slips and I hit the channel changer and there ya go, the golf channel is on."

Maude took another sip of her drink. "This is soo good!"

"Yeah!...Maybe I should order you another one."

"Oh, no, Dickie! I'll never get up in the morning, but that just reminded me of something. Did you ever call and complain about those two commercials that they're showing all the time?"

"What two commercials was that?" Dickie asked.

"You know, the two that tell you if you've had a hard-on for four hours to call your doctor. Who in their right mind will go walking in their doctors office with a hard-on?"

Dickie was shocked. "Maude, please keep your voice down. Everyone can hear you."

"I'm sorry but I just get so tired of those commercials. All those activists got rid of the cigarette ads and now the networks are selling pills to give you a hard-on. I bet they haven't even figured it out yet that that's why there's so many teenage pregnancies and that all those grandkids that never used to visit their grandparents are now visiting them once or twice a month and helping themselves to their grandpa's pills and he probably thinks he had memory loss."

"Oh, Maude! What am I going to do with you?"

The elderly couple seated at the table next to them got up to leave and as the man walked past their table, he stopped and spoke to Dickie.

Dickie's face was getting flushed. He looked up at the man and said, "Sir, I'm sorry. I think my wife has had a little too much to drink."

He looked at Dickie very seriously. "You know, I think your wife is right. All of a sudden our grandson has been visiting us every month and you can bet I'm going home and checking my pills." The man scratched his head. "Come to think of it, he's been in a real good mood lately." The old man walked away.

"I can't take you anywhere!" Dickie said as he finished his drink and looked at Maude.

"I want you to finish telling me about this golf channel and this Mr. Goosen. Who is he anyway?"

Maude looked up at Dickie and smiled. "He has the most gorgeous smile and I think he's very shy and let's see, what else do I know about him? Oh, yes, he's one of the top ranked golfers from South Africa and he and his wife just had a baby and he's another continent away and are you jealous yet?" Maude said laughing.

Dickie just sat there and looked at Maude.

Maude took a big sip of her drink and said, "Hey, you know what? I bet I could tell you who each golfer is from their butt."

Dickie just sat there stunned. He had never heard his beloved wife, his little angel of twenty years, talk like this.

"When we get home, young lady, you're getting blocked. Okay! I'll play your game. How can you tell the golfers by their rear end?"

Maude laughed and squirmed in her chair. "Each golfer has his own little wiggle before he putts and you know they have to bend over to putt."

"No, I wasn't aware of that. So what kind of a little wiggle does your dream boy have?"

"Well, that's what's really funny. He's the only one they never show from behind."

Dickie looked at Maude. Was she playing with him or what?

"Why is that? Why would he be the only one they never shoot from behind?"

"I don't know. They always shoot him from the side. Maybe he doesn't have a little wiggle, I don't know."

"Yes! I'm definitely going to have to block you," Dickie said as he watched Maude continue to sip her drink.

"So, tell me, how long has this been going on?"

"Well, I had to have something to do that was fun….It's like a little game that I play with myself….You know you work long hours and I get bored after awhile and kinda slip over to the golf channel. Hey, you know their Nick Faldo would be a great Inspector Clouseau. He's so funny! His hair sticks up like Peter Sellers' hair used to do and I just think that he would be wonderful and I'd even go to the show to see the movie. I should send Blake Edwards an e-mail and tell him!"

"I may have to commit you if you're not careful. So, what else is great about this golf channel?"

"I usually only watch it when Phil or Tiger is playing, but I really like the commercials, especially Tiger's with Charles Barkley."

"Who's Charles Barkley?"

"Dickie! You don't know who Charles Barkley is?"

Dickie shook his head. By this time, he was totally flabbergasted.

"Charles Barkley is one of the greatest basketball players that ever lived…and then there's Michael Jordan and Jerry West and of course Larry Bird… and back to golf. Sergio has a new commercial out that I really like.

He plays James Bond and he's really handsome and debonair in his elegant tuxedo and he really has a lot of hair that he keeps hidden under that baseball cap."

"So tell me, can you tell Sergio by his rear end?" Dickie asked, very agitated.

Maude took her last sip of her drink, looked Dickie straight in the eye, smiled and said, "Oh yes! He has the cutest little…" Before she could finish her sentence, Dickie jumped up and leaned over the table. "That's it! You sit right here until I go and pay the check and then we're outta here."

7

The morning sun streamed through the open windows in the garden room where Agnes hurriedly polished the silverware. The silverware had been in her family for decades; she was totally focused on making sure the silver maintained its highest quality of sheen. She held a fork out and inspected it. She then stuck it back into the silver polish, removed it and then continued to polish it until it glowed. She couldn't find her glasses again but she knew with the help of the sunlight that their silver would be shining when she was finished.

Their guests weren't arriving until the early afternoon so she could take her time and enjoy the warmth of the morning sun.

The door buzzer began to buzz persistently and made Agnes jump up out of her chair. She brushed her hair out of her face and walked to the front door.

She opened the door, jumped back and screamed, "Help! Help! Alice, where are you?"

She stood staring at the baby pumpkin person who just stood in the doorway staring at Agnes. The baby moved her head back and forth.

"Trick or Treat," the little pumpkin person said.

"Alice!...Alice!" Agnes began to scream.

A woman came running up the steps behind the baby to the front door.

"What's wrong?"

Alice came running up the steps from the cellar and walked up behind Agnes. They both stood there and stared at the baby pumpkin person. Alice held on to Agnes' shoulders.

A young voice could be heard from within the pumpkin head:

"Mommy! Can I take this thing off? It's too heavy!"

The mother put her hands on the pumpkin head and Alice and Agnes screamed.

"No!...No!"

The woman looked at Alice and Agnes and said, "You two look like you've seen a ghost?"

She removed the pumpkin head from the little girl and a beautiful blond girl smiled and said, "Trick or Treat!"

Alice and Agnes stood there staring at the girl.

Agnes finally spoke. "I thought she was our own little pumpkin person.

She's dressed just like her."

The woman laughed and said, "That was my idea. She wanted to have her picture made with your pumpkin people so I bought her clothes to match your little pumpkin people."

"How did you know what our pumpkin person was wearing?" Alice asked.

"Oh, I kinda snuck down here one night and checked it out. I hope you don't mind."

Alice and Agnes looked at each other. Alice spoke first; "Seems like someone's been asleep on the job!"

"Yes, I agree," Agnes said as she searched her apron for her glasses.

"We should take the pictures now because we're expecting company shortly," Alice said as she began to walk toward the back veranda.

"Yes, I agree," Agnes said as she followed her. The woman and child followed them to the back veranda and down the steps.

"Wow! Your pumpkin patch looks better in the daylight. Look how many pumpkins you have. Your pumpkin people look so realistic. How do you do it?" Her daughter gingerly patted one of the pumpkins.

"That's our big secret, isn't it, Alice?"

"Yes!" Alice said as she lovingly patted her pumpkins lying in the bed.

"Please stand beside the pumpkin bed and we'll take your picture," Agnes said.

The little girl put her pumpkin head on and then jumped in the bed with Alice and Agnes' pumpkin people. She stood next to the baby pumpkin person.

"No, you can't stand in there. Get out of there right now." Alice screamed.

The woman tried to pull her child out but she wouldn't move. "No, I want my picture taken here," the little girl said.

"Have her stand still and take her picture and then she must get out of the bed before she steps on my pumpkins."

The little girl put her arms around the baby pumpkin person and smiled for her mother. The mother held up the camera and pointed it at her daughter. "Okay, smile for the camera. This is going to be such a wonderful

Halloween picture, don't you think?" The woman heard the camera click and then she told her daughter to get out of the bed.

Alice and Agnes looked at each other. The little girl looked at the baby pumpkin person in the eyes and smiled.

The woman pulled her daughter from the bed, took her pumpkin head off and then looked in the screen of her camera to see if her picture came out.

She looked at the screen and then at the pumpkins again and again.

"Is there something wrong?" Alice asked.

"Well, I don't know. You look at the picture and you tell me. This is pretty amazing!"

Alice looked at the screen and then at Agnes. She tried to keep her composure and handed the camera to Agnes who looked at the screen.

"I need to get a better look at this," Agnes said as she froze in her footsteps and looked for her glasses. She fumbled through her pockets of her apron and finally found them. "Looks like you might have a trick camera."

Agnes put her glasses on and stared at the picture. All of their dear little pumpkins were smiling as the woman took their picture.

The woman looked at Agnes and then at the pumpkins. "No! I don't have a trick camera but look at the pumpkins now and look at them when I took the picture."

Agnes looked up at the sun and moved her finger to the erase button.

"I would say the sun was dancing off the pumpkins when you took the picture. It must have been a reflection from the pumpkin on the veranda."

Agnes handed the camera back to the woman and looked at Alice. The woman hurriedly put the camera into her bag.

"Alice, we have to get back to work before our guests arrive!"

Alice and Agnes began to walk around the side of the house and the woman and her child followed them.

"I don't see a pumpkin on the veranda, do you, sweetie?" the woman asked her daughter as they walked around the side of the house.

Alice and Agnes stopped in front of the steps and spoke to the woman.

"We have to get back to work because we have special guests arriving soon."

"I hope to see you next year," the woman said as she walked to her car.

She opened the door for her daughter, put her safely inside and then walked to the driver's door and opened it. "Happy Halloween!"

"Oh, yes, it will be!" Alice and Agnes said together and quietly walked up the steps to the front door.

"Boy that was close!" Agnes said as she followed her. They both walked in the front door and stopped.

Alice turned to Agnes. "Looks like we have a bunch of comedians out there in the pumpkin patch…Did you erase both the pictures?"

"Yes and a few more that she had on there when she snuck in here during the night. Wait till she finds out that she doesn't have any pictures."

"We've got to keep an eye out for her and we've got to make sure we close the gates from now on," Alice said defiantly, "because, somebody's sleeping on the job."

Alice returned to the cellar and Agnes returned to finish her task of polishing the family silverware. She had just sat down and had picked up a fork when the buzzer rang again.

"What's with people today? I can't get my job done." She laid the fork down, took her glasses off, laid them down on the table and slowly walked to the front door.

Agnes was faced with a distraught looking woman.

"Can I help you?" Agnes asked her.

"I'm Rebecca…Remember? Rebecca? I was here with my husband, Harold, he disappeared!"

Agnes stared at the woman's face and then said, "Oh yes, now I remember."

"I apologize for showing up without a reservation, but I'm just beside myself. Harold hasn't called or sent me a note and the police aren't doing anything and I know he's out there somewhere."

"Yes, I see! Why don't you come in and I'll make us some tea."

"If you're sure it's no bother," Rebecca said as she walked into the garden room. She sat down at the table where Agnes had been working.

"I'll just yell for Alice and then I'll make us some tea", Agnes said as she walked into the kitchen.

Agnes yelled for Alice and then remembered that she was in the cellar. She walked over to the cellar door, opened it and yelled.

"Alice! We have company. You better come up!"

Five minutes later Alice came walking out the door, her hair disheveled, looking frazzled.

"Agnes, you mixed the jars again."

"No, I didn't."

"Yes, you did and I'm telling you that you need to start wearing your glasses and what's all the commotion about now?"

"We have company," Agnes said and motioned toward the garden room.

Alice turned to look in the garden room. She saw Rebecca standing at the window gazing out at the ocean and sipping a cup of tea. Agnes whispered in Alice's ear, "She's still looking for her husband and she's been to the police again."

"Really!" Alice watched Rebecca and then turned toward Agnes. "Did you make her a cup of regular tea or our special tea?"

"Well, I kinda made the special tea since she said she'd been to the police again."

"Well, I think we should give Harold to her and then get rid of her for good, don't you?"

"Yes! That would be fun," Agnes said as she rubbed her hands together.

They walked into the garden room together and stopped behind Rebecca.

"Well, I see we have a visitor," Alice said as Rebecca turned around to face them.

"I'm sorry to bother you again, but, I just don't know what to do and the police aren't doing anything and I'm just going crazy. Harold has never done anything like this in his life and I thought maybe he had come back here since he liked this place so much!"

Alice smiled and said, "No, we haven't seen him. He's so young and athletic maybe he decided to go fishing or run a marathon or something."

"But he would have told me if he was going to do that," Rebecca said as she sat down at the table very slowly. "All of a sudden I feel very tired."

Alice and Agnes looked at each other. "You never know about these young guys. Anyway, we were getting ready to have a bowl of stew and I remember that you liked stew, didn't you?"

"Yes!"

"Agnes, why don't you run down to the cellar and get a jar of stew for Rebecca."

Agnes began to look for her glasses in the pockets of her apron.

"Agnes, we don't have all day so hurry along," Alice said in a defiant tone.

"Oh, all right," Agnes said as she walked to the cellar door and down the steps. "I don't know why I always have to get the jars."

Agnes turned the light on and walked to the aisle marked H in big letters. "Oh, no, Alice took all the labels off." She tried to figure out which jar was which. "Let's see! Henry, Harriet, Homer, Hank, Hans."

She heard Alice yelling for her. "What am I going to do?" She scratched her head and grabbed a jar. "Does it really matter?" She ran up the steps.

Agnes hurriedly poured the contents of the jar in a pan and heated it while Alice removed the silverware from the table and sat down.

Rebecca walked slowly to the table. "I don't know what's wrong with me.

All of a sudden I'm so tired."

Alice smiled at her. "Why don't you sit down and we'll have our stew.

Rebecca sat down across from Alice. "I need to check on our stew. I'll be right back."

Alice walked into the kitchen just as Agnes finished pouring the stew into a bowl.

"We need to hurry. She's already on her way out," Alice said laughing.

She opened the cabinet door and pulled out a jar of olives and picked two out; putting them on top of the stew.

"I think we're ready," Agnes said as she picked up the tray and carried it to the table. She set it down in front of Rebecca.

Rebecca looked at the stew and screamed.

"What is it?" Alice asked.

"There are two eyeballs in my stew!"

Alice and Agnes both looked in the bowl of stew.

Agnes picked one of the olives out of the stew and popped it in her mouth and laughed and said, "They're only olives, Rebecca."

"Oh! Silly me!" Rebecca said as she took a big spoonful of stew.

Alice and Agnes both sat there smiling at her, watching her eat the stew.

"Aren't you going to have anything to eat?" Rebecca asked.

"No! We ate while we were preparing it for you," Alice said.

"Ohhhhhh!"

"Besides, it's fun just to sit and watch," Agnes said laughing.

Alice hit Agnes under the table and she moaned as they watched Rebecca eat another spoonful of stew.

"What happened?"

"Nothing! She's always banging herself or something."

Rebecca stopped eating and stuck her finger in her mouth.

"What's wrong?" Alice asked.

Rebecca didn't answer. She kept digging in her mouth until she pulled a bright red fingernail out and held it in front of her face. She screamed.

"It's a fingernail." She dropped it on the table.

Alice and Agnes held out their hands and looked at their fingernails.

"It's not mine!" Alice said as she looked at Agnes hands.

"It's not mine, either. It's not even my color."

Rebecca stood up and grabbed the table to stop her from swaying. She grabbed her stomach and then ran out the back door and into the pumpkin patch.

Alice and Agnes jumped up from the table to follow Rebecca but Alice turned to speak to Agnes. "Looks like you got the wrong jar again."

"Well!...You took all the labels off so I had to pick one and besides you didn't give me time to find my glasses."

"Looks like you better hurry out and see where she's gone."

Agnes hurried out the back door to find Rebecca. She found her bent over their special pumpkin bed ready to throw up.

"No, you can't throw up there."

She moved Rebecca over behind the pumpkin beds next to the pumpkin people. Agnes pulled out her cell phone, pushed the button and waited for Alice to answer.

Rebecca saw the phone and stood up.

"That's Harold's phone!"

"No, it's not! It's mine."

"No, it's not! Give it to me," Rebecca screamed as she grabbed Agnes and tried to take the phone from her. In an instant Alice was by Agnes' side.

"What's going on here?" Alice asked Rebecca.

She's got Harold's phone and I want it back."

"You can't have it back. It belongs to Agnes."

Agnes smiled and said, "See! I told you it was my phone."

"What did you do to Harold? I'm going to call the police," Rebecca screamed as she backed away from them.

"Oh, no you're not!" Alice said as she walked closer to Rebecca.

"I'm calling the cops," she said as she tried to get around the pumpkin bed but Alice stood in front of her.

She jumped behind the special pumpkin bed and tried to hide behind the pumpkin people. "Now, you've really made a big mistake," Alice said.

"What do you mean?" She looked around and didn't see anyone but them and the pumpkin people.

"You're surrounded, Rebecca," Alice said very quietly.

"What are you talking about? There's no one here but two old biddies and a bunch of old pumpkin scarecrows"

Alice turned to Agnes and said, "Why is it that people are always throwing the age bit into a conversation?"

"I don't know. It doesn't seem fair, does it?" Agnes said as she put her cell in her apron pocket.

"You two have lost your marbles and I'm going to tell!"

"Who are you going to tell? There's no one here that cares," Alice said as she walked around to the front of the pumpkin patch.

"Boys, I think we need to teach Rebecca a lesson." "Boys, who are you talking to?" Rebecca asked.

Alice looked at her and smiled. "I suppose you never saw the Wizard of Oz?"

"The what? Now I know you've lost it," Rebecca said as she tried to push her way past Alice.

Alice stopped her and the pumpkin man grabbed Rebecca's arm and pulled her back.

Rebecca looked down in horror at the arm holding her and then up at the smiling face staring at her. She tried to pull her arm away but the pumpkin man held on.

"It's the tea, isn't it? It's making me hallucinate? This isn't really happening to me, is it?" she cried.

Agnes stared at her and said, "You should be nice to your elders, dearie!"

Rebecca turned to look the pumpkin man in the eyes and asked. "Harold is that you?" The pumpkin man stared at Rebecca and laughed before he said, "No!"

"You buried Harold in one of your pumpkin beds didn't you?" Rebecca screamed as she tried to pull her arm away.

Alice spoke up first. "No, he wasn't good enough. We take only the finest ingredients and he certainly wasn't that."

Rebecca kicked the pumpkin man in the leg. As he reached for his leg she was finally able to pull her arm free. She began running toward the cliff.

"Help, Help!" she cried.

"Run! Run! There's no one here to help you. You have no place to hide. You should have never come back," Alice said as she walked closer.

The pumpkin family followed Alice and Agnes to the edge of the cliff.

"I just needed to know where Harold is. You aren't really going to hurt me, are you?" Rebecca cried as she took one more step closer to the edge of the cliff.

"We've told you that Harold isn't here. We only take the best and he didn't even come close," Agnes said with a smile.

"Agnes, our guest will be arriving soon so we must get back to work," Alice said with delight.

"It's time to say good-bye Rebecca. Boys, you know what to do,"

Alice said to the pumpkin family. She turned her back to Rebecca and began to walk away.

"Wait! You can't leave me here," Rebecca screamed.

Alice and Agnes turned around and smiled and said, "We didn't plan on it!"

8

Dickie pulled the drapes back from the windows so the morning sunlight could flow into the room.

"Ohhhhh! Ohhhhh! Dickie! The sun is making too much noise."

Maude slowly lifted her head from the pillow. "My head is spinning."

Dickie walked across the room to the bathroom and returned with a glass of Coke.

"Here! Drink this because it will make you feel better."

Maude slowly pulled her body up and took the glass from Dickie. "What happened? Did I eat dinner last night?"

"Let's just say that you ate your dinner and everyone else's."

"What?" Maude screamed. "Ohhhh! That hurt."

"I was only kidding. Yes, you ate your dinner but I think that you had a few too many pomegranate martinis."

"I don't remember leaving the restaurant. How did you get me back to the hotel?"

"You walked on your own. Don't you remember that you were singing up a storm with the reggae band as we walked by and everyone wanted you to stop and sing with them?"

"Ohhhhh! Don't tell me that. I'm sorry! Maybe a shower would help me feel better." Maude finished drinking the coke. She got up and slowly walked into the bathroom.

"Yes. Why don't you take a shower and I'll just sit here and watch TV." Dickie sat down on the edge of the bed and reached for the remote control. "Take your time and then we'll go eat."

Maude closed the door to the bathroom. When he could hear the water running, Dickie clicked the TV on to the golf channel. He sat there staring at the golfers.

Maude surprised him as she opened the door to the bathroom. "Dickie, is that Nick Faldo that I hear talking?"

Dickie quickly pressed the button for the TV and turned it off. "Who's Nick Faldo?"

"He's the announcer for the golf channel. Were you watching the golf channel?"

"No! I was looking for the food network and I was just flipping the channels."

"Ohhhhh," Maude said as she closed the door and smiled.

Dickie listened for a minute and then turned the TV back on. He watched the golfers play for a few minutes and then turned it off and got up and walked across the room to the balcony and walked outside. He took in a deep breath of fresh air and stared at the ocean.

Maude came out of the bathroom a short time later and was ready to go and have breakfast.

She walked over to Dickie and put her arms around him and gave him a big hug and looked up into his eyes. "You're great to put up with me and my martinis. Suppose you let me buy you breakfast."

"Well, you must be feeling better," Dickie said with a faint smile.

"Yes! A wonderful shower is the best remedy, don't you think?" she said as she smiled at Dickie.

"We need to eat and then hit the road. What time did you tell Agnes that we would be at the Pumpkin Patch?"

"I told her early afternoon because she wanted to make sure that we had time for a cup of tea before dinner. Wasn't that sweet of her?"

"Yes! Sweet old Agnes!"

"Now, Dickie, you have to be nice to Agnes if you plan on stealing her recipe and one of her itty, bitty pumpkins."

"I'm just praying that this recipe is the best so that I'll win the pastry challenge. Who knows, maybe I'll get my own show."

"Dickie, you have enough to do already with the restaurant. How could you handle all that stress?"

"I don't know. It's just a thought. First things first! Let's go check out of the hotel and then go eat and then head out toward Monterey."

"It sounds like a plan to me," Maude said as she began to pack her bag.

She looked at Dickie and watched him folding his clothes.

"Dickie! Are you ready for a change in your life?"

"What do you mean?"

"Are you serious about wanting to do a food network show on TV?"

Dickie scratched his head, sat down on the side of the bed and looked at Maude. "I don't know. Maybe I need a change. I'm not sure what I need but we'll figure it out together and go from there."

9

Maude took a deep breath of fresh air as they drove up the coast highway. She was beginning to feel a lot better since she had breakfast and couldn't wait until they reached Monterey.

Dickie sat behind the wheel of his little red convertible sports car. He loved to drive on roads like the coast highway with all the twists and turns. Maude had given the Triumph to him as a gift for winning his first Cookie Cutter Competition. He practically slept in it every night to make sure no one touched his precious little car.

Maude was so happy that he was pleased with the super little Triumph because she had spent a great deal of time and money getting the car in good condition. The body of the car was in good shape, so all she had to do was to get the car repainted a bright, shiny, fire-engine red which was Dickie's favorite color. She had all the upholstery and panel work replaced and the biggest surprise of all was the gearshift that she had designed like a cupcake. This was going to be the best gift that she had ever given him and it had to be perfect because it was going to be the first brand new car that Dickie had ever owned.

Dickie had always driven secondhand cars because he spent all his time and money on cuisine classes and pastry lessons to keep him on top of his career as a pastry chef.

The only gift that Maude and Dickie had ever given themselves in their twenty years of marriage was their new home and each other. They pushed themselves to be their best at their jobs and didn't spend a lot of time socializing but when they did, it was together. They were the ultimate couple, the best husband and wife team that were also best friends. Each had their own career but faced the challenge of their spouse's career as their own.

When Dickie would have too much sugar during the day he would often wonder what he would do without Maude. Why the sugar affected him, he didn't know, but he knew that he could never be without her.

As he drove up the coast his thoughts went back to their conversation last night in the restaurant. So she watched the golf channel a lot. Hmmm!

"Dickie! What are you thinking about? You look so serious."

Dickie could feel his face turning red. "Nothing!"

"Well, why is your face turning red?"

He had to think fast. "If you must know, I was thinking about what we're going to do tonight since you were a little out of it last night."

Maude didn't expect him to answer that because she knew exactly what he was thinking about. She knew her little act about the pro golfers really woke him up and she knew it definitely took his mind off his upcoming competition.

"And, I was thinking that when we get home that maybe I'll take some golf lessons. You know, you've been bugging me for years to play with you and I was thinking that maybe I spend too much time at work and that I should take a day off to do something with you."

"What brought this on?" Maude said trying to keep from laughing as she turned to look at Dickie.

"I don't know. I was thinking that maybe I spend too much time at work trying to be the best. Every time that we do something it pertains to my job; and we haven't done anything in years together that was just for us."

Maude couldn't believe what she was hearing. She stared at Dickie and smiled.

"Okay! What's the catch?"

"What do you mean?"

"You despise golf. Remember? People are crazy for chasing a little white ball around acres of grass. Do you remember saying that? Why do you want to play with me now?"

"Maude it doesn't have to be golf. You've always wanted to go to a Lakers game and I've always had some excuse because I don't like sports like you do. But I just realized that we've been married twenty years and we don't take time to just relax together. It's always about your job or about my job and I think that we need to start taking time together before it's too late.

Every time we have company, it's from your work or mine and I think we need to just enjoy ourselves, just the two of us."

Maude was flabbergasted. Tears came to her eyes; she didn't speak for a minute. She let the wind gently hit her in the face as they sped toward Monterey.

A few minutes later Maude turned toward Dickie and said, "Dickie, I love you!" That's all Maude could say at that moment.

Dickie turned toward Maude for a second and said, "I love you too. You're my heart and soul."

10

Dickie turned the car into the drive for The Pumpkin Patch Bed and Breakfast and drove a few feet into the road past the gate and then stopped.

He couldn't believe his eyes.

"It's breathtaking!" Maude said as she gasped at the beauty of the pumpkin fields and the glimmering sun shining on the bed and breakfast.

"Look! There's a golden rainbow over the house. Do you see it?"

Dickie sat there mesmerized; it was like a fairy tale come true.

"Oh, my word, I've never seen anything so beautiful," Maude said.

"Look at all the thousands of pumpkins everywhere. Look! They're twinkling. It looks like they're happy to see us."

Dickie opened his door and got out to enjoy the most spectacular sight that he had ever seen. "This is sensational," he said as he looked at the magnificent fields. "I've never seen such beauty in a pumpkin field before and I hope that just one of them is waiting for me."

Just as Dickie finished his sentence, a squad car approached from the road to the house. The sun must have shielded it from sight because Dickie had not seen it.

As the car got closer, Maude and Dickie waved and the car stopped.

The sergeant stuck his head out of the window and said, "You must be Maude and Dickie."

"Yes! How did you know?" Maude asked.

"Alice and Agnes told me they were expecting special guest this evening and the way that you're looking at the pumpkin fields makes me think that you would be them."

Dickie laughed and said, "Guilty as charged."

The sergeant finished by saying, "I've been coming to the Bed and Breakfast for years just to eat their delicious pumpkin bread. If you ask me, it's to die for." The sergeant laughed and then said, "Enjoy yourself! Alice and Agnes are waiting for you." He waved goodbye and drove out the gates to the end of the driveway.

"Do you think he could tell what we're up to?"

Dickie smiled as he looked at Maude and said, "There's no way. Besides, he looks like he just woke up from a nap. Anyway, I just can't believe that this place is so beautiful and that two elderly sisters take care of it. We shouldn't have any problems getting the recipe and taking one of these pumpkins. Heck, they have tons of pumpkins. How would they know if one was missing?"

"We'll just have to be very careful. Besides, this place is magical. I've never seen a pumpkin glow. The next thing we'll know is that they'll all be smiling at us. Hey, today is Halloween. Wouldn't that be a riot?" They got in the car and Dickie started it up; they slowly drove toward the house.

"Dickie! Look at all the pumpkin people. They look so real. Look at the clothes they're wearing. She looks like she's wearing Gloria Vanderbilt jeans. Wow! It must cost them a fortune to put clothes like that on scarecrows."

Just then, Maude felt a sudden chill come over her shoulders.

"What's wrong?" Dickie asked.

"I don't know. All of a sudden I felt a big cold chill that gave me goose bumps."

Dickie laughed. "You're just getting nervous because tonight you and I become thieves."

"No! That's you become a thief and I become an accomplice!"

"Whichever way, I all of a sudden feel relaxed. Isn't that strange? Maude you're the cutest little thief that I've ever seen."

Dickie pulled up in front of The Pumpkin Patch bed and Breakfast to find Alice and Agnes standing on the front porch waiting for them.

Alice and Agnes shouted together, "Hello!"

Maude and Dickie waved and got out of their car and walked up to the porch.

"I know you must be Dickie and I have been anxiously waiting to meet you. I understand that you're a fantastic pastry chef," Agnes said as she shook hands with Dickie.

Dickie smiled, looked at Maude. He thought that the cat was out of the bag. Now, they would be watching him for sure.

Alice shook hands with Maude and smiled. "While they compare recipes, you and I can stroll the pumpkin fields."

"That would be great. I have never seen such beautiful pumpkins before in my life. They just seem to glow. How do you do it?"

Alice laughed and said, "That's our secret ingredient. Agnes and I have kept that in our family for years. Isn't that right?"

Agnes smiled at Alice and then suggested they move into the house. "Why don't we get you settled and then we can have a cup of tea and some of our wonderful pumpkin bread."

"I can't wait to taste your pumpkin bread," Dickie replied as he looked at his precious car. "Is it okay to leave my car here?"

"Yes! We'll close the gates so that no one can enter and your car will be okay right where it is," Alice said. "You can't ever tell what's going to happen on Halloween night." She motioned for Agnes to lead the way.

Once they entered the house, Alice went to the control box and closed the gate.

"The gates are closed so you don't have to worry about your car."

"Agnes! Why don't you show Maude and Dickie to their room while I make some tea!"

"Follow me and I'll take you upstairs to your room with a spectacular view."

"I can't wait," Maude said as she followed Agnes. Dickie picked up their luggage and followed them.

Agnes led them into the upstairs bedroom that faced the ocean and the special pumpkin patches.

Maude walked over to the open window and looked out the window toward the ocean and then down to the pumpkin gardens. She then turned to face Agnes. "This view is spectacular. Dickie, you must come and take a look at it."

Dickie sat their luggage on the floor and walked over to stand beside Maude. "Oh, my word, what a view! This view is to die for."

"Well, we don't want you to do that," Agnes said as she laughed and walked toward the door. "I'll let you guys freshen up and then come downstairs so we can have tea and pumpkin bread and talk. But, before I go, there is a gold plate here for you to put your cell phone on while you're here. We're sorry but we just got really tired of hearing them ring, especially at night, so we made a rule, No cell phones!"

"That's okay by us, we need the rest," Maude said as she reached in her purse for the cell. She walked over and put it on the gold plate. Agnes looked at the phone, smiled and walked out the door.

"Thank you so much," Maude said as she closed the door to their room and walked over to Dickie.

"Just look at those pumpkins, Dickie. Don't they look wonderful?"

"Why did you tell her I was a pastry chef? She'll be watching me the whole time we're here?"

"I didn't tell her that you were a chef. That would have blown our whole deal. I don't know how she knew. But, I don't think that we have to worry. They aren't spring chickens anymore and I bet when they go to bed that they conk out."

"This is going to drive me crazy. If you didn't tell her, then who did?"

Dickie leaned out the window. "Look! There's a trellis running down the side of the house." He leaned out and shook the trellis to see if it was sturdy enough to climb down and then back up.

Maude leaned out the window to see the trellis. "Let's freshen up and then go down and maybe we'll find out how she knew," Maude said as she headed for the bathroom.

"Maude, you look like you're getting tense. Maybe you should take a bubble bath or something to relax you after we have tea and pumpkin bread."

"Yes! That sounds like a great idea, especially since there is a big, beautiful tub in here just waiting for me. It looks like it has my name on it."

As the evening sun began its slow descent, Alice and Agnes were hurriedly preparing the special herb tea as Maude and Dickie entered the garden room.

"Please sit on the veranda and we'll bring the tea out to you," Agnes said as she placed the cups on the tray.

"I have never seen anything so spectacular as these pumpkin gardens. You ladies must have a million helpers to help keep them looking like this."

"No! It's just the two of us," Alice replied with a big grin. "We work pretty fast for old ladies."

"That's why we don't have a lot of company; we pick the cream of the crop, so to speak, when we have guests," Agnes said as Alice walked over next to her and poked her in the arm.

Alice walked out onto the veranda and turned to face Dickie and Maude. "Why don't I show you our special pumpkin beds before the sun goes down while we wait for Agnes to finish the tea and bread."

"Oh, yes that would be wonderful," Dickie said as he jumped up from his chair. He turned to look at Maude as she got up from her chair.

Alice walked down the steps with Dickie and Maude into the pumpkin garden; the pumpkins looked like they were glowing in the afternoon sun.

"The pumpkins look like they're twinkling in the sunshine," Maude said as she stared at the baby pumpkin person.

"Alice, I just don't know how you two can take care of this huge place.

Your pumpkins look lush, healthy and scrumptious." He leaned over to inspect the leaves. "I don't see any little critters on any of the leaves."

"I have to tell you that Agnes and I fall in bed at night sometimes, but, we love to take care of the pumpkin fields and especially these special gardens."

"What makes them special?" Dickie asked.

"That's our secret ingredient beds and I can't tell because then it wouldn't be our secret, would it?"

Dickie looked around to see where Maude was; she was up ahead staring at the baby pumpkin person.

"Maude, what are you staring at?"

"I could have sworn that this baby pumpkin person smiled at me."

Dickie laughed and looked at Alice who was still staring at the baby pumpkin person.

Alice walked up to where Maude was standing and stared at the baby.

Agnes yelled for them to come and have tea.

"Maude, I think it's just the sun shining on the pumpkins, that's all,"

Alice said. A black cat jumped up on the arm of the man pumpkin person.

"Kitty, where have you been?"

"Wow! That cat sure is strong to jump all the way up there." Dickie said as he watched the cat curl around the man's arm. "We had better go have tea before it gets too cold to drink," Alice said as she walked toward the steps. Just as Dickie turned around to follow her, he heard the cat screech and turned to see it lying on the ground as if it had been knocked off the arm of the pumpkin person. Little did he know that the pumpkin man had indeed knocked the cat off of his arm.

12

The afternoon sun was fading fast as Maude and Dickie sat in the rattan rocking chairs facing the special pumpkin beds. When the afternoon sun glistened over the pumpkins, they looked as though they were sprinkled with gold and that they were basking in the sunlight.

Alice walked out onto the veranda carrying a tray loaded with pumpkin bread and Agnes followed her carrying the tray with their special herb tea.

Agnes gave Maude and Dickie a cup of tea and then Alice sat the tray of pumpkin bread on the rattan table sitting between them.

"Eat as much as you want but don't forget we still have to have dinner and we're having a rack of lamb that we got just for you. It's not often that we get a chef as a guest." Agnes watched Dickie slowly chew the pumpkin bread as if he was trying to determine what ingredients were in the bread.

When Dickie finished chewing his bread he looked at Agnes and said, "I have to tell you that this bread is fantastic. I've never tasted anything so good. I've never seen the inside of pumpkin bread look so blood red! How do you do it?"

Alice and Agnes just smiled and said, "That's our secret ingredient."

"How did you know that Dickie was a chef?" Maude asked as she looked at Alice and then at Agnes.

Alice and Agnes looked at each other as if they were trying to decide what their answer should be.

Alice finally spoke up. "Agnes is always surfing the Internet and she continually checks the food network to see if any new recipes have come up that we would like. And that's where she saw Dickies name and it rang a bell because when he won the Golden Banana Award, we went crazy trying to make Golden Bananas with pumpkin. And no matter how we baked them, they didn't taste very good so we were hoping that Dickie would show us how to do that while you're here."

"Yes and we went and bought all the ingredients for you yesterday," Agnes said.

Dickie was shocked that two little old ladies would want him to cook for them. He looked at Maude. He could feel his face turning red.

"We didn't mean to embarrass you and I know this is your vacation but we would be very happy if you could do this for us tomorrow."

"I don't see why not. Maybe, you'll tell me how you cook this fabulous bread in the meantime."

"Oh, no you don't. You're a sly one, aren't you?" Alice said as she headed in the house.

Agnes turned around to follow her and then stopped as Maude made the statement. "I bet this is why the police were here."

"What do you mean?" Agnes asked as she turned to face the pumpkin beds.

"The pumpkin bread! You know how cops like to eat."

"Oh, no! That's not why he was here."

Alice heard them talking and came back out to the veranda just in time to hear Agnes say, "A woman jumped off the cliff. She was sad and lonely."

"Agnes, don't bore our guest."

"That's too bad!" Maude replied as she took another sip of tea.

"Yeah! Her husband disappeared and she came back here hoping that her husband had come back to see us. She just wanted some thread of hope.

We should have known that she was really depressed. We thought she had left and went back to tending to our pumpkins and the next thing you know, the sergeant is knocking on the door."

Alice walked over to stand beside Agnes. "That's another reason why we want to keep the gate closed."

Agnes laughed and said, "Yeah, the sergeant always finds a reason to come here so that he can have tea and pumpkin bread."

"We saw him leaving as we were coming in, looked like he had taken a nap," Dickie said as he yawned. "I don't know what's wrong with me. All of a sudden, I feel sleepy."

"Why don't you two go take a short nap and we'll get dinner going," Agnes said as she walked toward the door with Alice following her.

13

Maude and Dickie layed down on the bed. Maude yawned and rolled over to face Dickie. "This is a wonderful place, isn't it?... I don't know why I'm so tired all of a sudden."

"Me either, but, I just know that I'm going to get my award winning dessert from here. By the way, did you bring your big bag?"

"Yes! It's in my case. We have to be very careful and quiet." Maude yawned again and saw Dickie close his eyes. She rolled over to face the door and closed her eyes and was sound sleep.

The bedroom door opened slowly. Agnes peeked around the door and then walked in very quietly with Alice following her. They stood at the dresser looking at the cell phone.

Agnes whispered to Alice, "I want this phone because it has a cat on it."

"I thought it was my turn to get the phone;" Alice replied.

Agnes whispered, "No! It was your turn the last time."

"No! It was your turn the last time."

"No, it wasn't. It's my turn."

Maude opened her eyes and looked at them. They stood still and looked at her. Maude closed her eyes again and rolled over. Alice and Agnes tiptoed out of the room and closed the door after Agnes picked up the cell phone.

When they reached the kitchen, Agnes opened the cell to see how many minutes were on the phone. "Looks like she never uses this phone, it's got a full charge, so I'm going to call Henry and see what he's doing.

Do you want to call your cousin in Minnesota?"

Alice picked four plates out of the cabinet and set them on the counter. "No, I don't think I will this time, maybe later."

Agnes walked up behind Alice humming. Alice turned to face her and said, "Stop humming, you're driving me crazy."

"I'm just excited about this phone. I love cats. You know that." She opened the phone again to hear the ring and started humming.

"You need to hurry up and use the phone and put it back before they wake up," Alice said as she worked on the lamb shank.

"Won't Dickie be surprised when he finds out what we've got in store for him," Agnes said as she dialed the phone.

"Shhhh!" Alice said as she turned around to look in the room.

Agnes stared at the phone and said, "That's so strange. I still can't get Henry on the phone. He hasn't been answering all day. Didn't you tell him that we're having special guests this weekend?"

"Yes! He's probably taking care of a few loose ends and he'll be here soon."

"Did you give him the new code to the gate?" Agnes asked as she put the cell back in her pocket.

"Yes and you'd better go put the phone back because they won't sleep long," Alice said as she shook the jar of special herb tea. "We're running out of our special tea so I hope he's running the errands I told him to."

Maude and Dickie woke up an hour later and lay there, looking at the ceiling.

Maude looked at Dickie and said, "I had the craziest dream!"

"What was that?" Dickie asked.

Maude raised herself up to look at the dresser and the gold plate. Her cell phone was still sitting on it. She laughed.

"I dreamed that Alice and Agnes were standing over there over the cell phone arguing about who got the phone this time."

Dickie laughed and got up. He went to the window and looked out at the pumpkin patch.

"I just know the secret is out there with the pumpkins. I've just got to figure out how."

"Well, if you ask me, you better watch out for the pumpkin people. I would swear that that pumpkin baby was staring at me like I was its lost mother or something."

Dickie stood gazing at the special pumpkin field shining under the floodlight. "The taste has to be in those special pumpkin beds. If I could take just one of the little ones, I would have enough to make my pumpkin bread and I know that I could make the taste so scrumptious that it would be an award winner."

"I'm curious! Why do they call it a Golden Spatula Award when you're baking?"

"I don't know. I've never really thought about it. Maybe it's because you have to stir the batter with a spatula. Who knows? I just want to win."

Maude got up and walked to the window. She put her arm around Dickie's shoulders and looked out at the pumpkin patch.

"I think that I can sneak down the trellis tonight and pick one of the small ripe pumpkins and then climb back up the trellis. We can put it in your bag and hide it in the luggage and they won't suspect a thing…I think that I have the perfect pumpkin picked out."

"All I can say is that you better watch out for those pumpkin people. They give me the creeps."

Dickie laughed and kissed Maude. He walked toward the bathroom.

"You worry too much. We had better freshen up and get downstairs because I can smell the lamb shank cooking and we don't want to keep out host waiting."

Maude stood there looking at the special pumpkin patch. Just as she was ready to turn around she thought she saw the baby move. She stared at the baby.

"What are you looking at?" Dickie asked as he walked into the bedroom.

"I could have sworn the baby scarecrow moved."

Dickie walked to the window and looked out. "I don't see any movement. It was probably just the wind from the ocean." He hugged Maude and said, "You're probably just tense about the crime we are about to commit!"

Maude looked at Dickie and then looked back at the baby. She turned to walk into the bathroom. "I'll just be a minute."

Dickie walked away from the window just as the baby pumpkin person looked up in their direction.

14

Maude and Dickie walked into the dining room as Alice and Agnes were putting the food on the table.

"This is perfect timing. Did you sleep well?" Agnes asked.

"Oh, yes! We conked out really fast," Maude replied.

Just then, the telephone rang and Agnes walked over to answer it. She picked up the receiver.

"Hello! Hello!"

She put her hand over the phone and talked to Alice. "It's the Bargain Basement. No! We don't have a donation yet. Maybe, in a few days…Okay! We'll call you." Agnes hung up the phone.

"Everyone sit down to eat," Alice said.

"Where do you want us to sit?" Maude asked.

Agnes stood behind the chair that faced the door. "I always sit here and Alice always sits next to me, so you can sit over there."

Dickie and Maude sat down at the Table. "This looks and smells wonderful."

Dickie added, "Yes, it does."

"Well! I'm sure it's not as good as what you prepare, but the more that we practice, the better it gets. Isn't that right, Agnes?"

"Yes and we hope that you like it," Agnes added.

Alice and Agnes smiled at Maude and Dickie as he sat there staring at the big plate of pumpkin bread that was sitting right in front of him.

"You have to tell me how you get the pumpkin bread so red," Dickie said as he stared at the bread."

Alice looked at Agnes and then replied, "That's part of our secret."

"It tastes like nothing that I've ever eaten before," Dickie said as he devoured his leg of lamb.

"I would say so," Alice said with a wry smile.

"Does it take you a long time to bake it?" Maude asked.

Agnes replied, "I wouldn't say it takes a long time to bake it, it takes a long time to……Ouch!" Alice had kicked Agnes under the table. They looked at each other.

Alice continued, "This recipe has been in our family for a long time."

"I see!" Dickie said as he helped himself to a piece of pumpkin bread. "I can't wait to taste this again."

As he slowly chewed the bread, Dickie said, "This has cinnamon…um…nutmeg…I can taste a little bit of molasses and I think a little bit of ginger and I know that it's not food coloring that's making it red but I just can't put my finger on it."

"Agnes, we should clear the table," Alice said. She got up and walked around to Dickie's side of the table. She dropped a knife so that it hit

Dickie's arm.

"Ouch!"

"Oh, I'm so sorry," she said as she quickly wiped the blood with her finger. She then stuck the finger in her mouth and sucked the blood.

"Ummm!" Alice said as she headed for the kitchen.

Agnes jumped up from the table and said, "I'll get you a band-aid."

She ran off to the cupboard and came back with a band-aid. She put it on Dickie's arm.

"There! That should fix you up."

"That's all right. I think that another piece of bread will make me feel just fine."

Agnes handed Dickie the platter of bread. She picked up a plate and headed for the kitchen. She walked over to Alice who was standing there smiling.

"He's perfect," she whispered.

They walked back into the dining room smiling as they saw Dickie eating another piece of bread and Maude having another cup of tea.

Alice suggested that they move out to the veranda and have more bread and tea.

Maude said she loved the tea and to make a big pot of it.

"You guys go ahead and sit on the veranda and we'll be right out."

Maude and Dickie again sat down on the rockers and waited for Alice and Agnes to come out. Shortly, they came out carrying the tea tray filled with more pumpkin bread and special herbal tea.

Agnes poured tea for everyone and sat down. Dickie took a drink of his tea while staring at the pumpkins. Alice watched Dickie.

Maude closed her eyes as she breathed in the aroma of the tea.

Alice suggested to Dickie that she show him the special pumpkins in their special beds on their Kitty Cat Path.

Dickie was excited to get a closer look at those special pumpkins, so he jumped up and followed Alice down the steps and out into the pumpkin garden. Kitty sat on the top step watching Dickie as he followed Alice.

"What do you feed Kitty?" Maude asked.

"Oh, we don't feed him. He's never hungry."

"Oh!" Maude said as Agnes got up and poured her another cup of tea.

"What did the cop want earlier?"

"What…did…the…cop…want? I thought that I had told you."

Agnes had opened the front door to see the Sergeant standing there. He wanted to come in so Agnes opened the door; he walked to the back veranda and looked out toward the cliff.

When he asked if Alice was there he seemed very serious; she got very nervous and decided to make him some tea.

She made him some special herb tea and sat down with him while he drank it. He emptied the teacup, looked at Agnes, closed his eyes and went to sleep.

Agnes took the cup out of his hands and sat it on the table; she tiptoed to the back of the house to find Alice.

"Alice, the Sergeant is here," Agnes said as she walked in the bedroom.

"Well! Invite him in."

"I did!"

Alice looked up at Agnes and said, "And what?"

"Well, I gave him a cup of tea and he fell asleep."

"You did what?" Alice said as she hurried out of the room with Agnes hurrying behind her.

Alice slowly walked toward the sergeant. Agnes followed.

She whispered, "Which tea did you give him?"

Agnes fidgeted with her apron string and said, "I don't know. I just picked up the pot and poured the tea."

Alice scratched her head; she put her hands on her hips. Agnes put her hands on her hips and stared at her sister.

"Okay…I think that we had better run his watch back. How long has he been out?"

"Probably twenty minutes."

Alice picked up his wrist and ran his watch back an hour.

"What got you so bummed out?"

"I don't know! I guess I was afraid he was going to ask me some more questions."

"Like what?"

"You know, like how come Rebecca had come back here and how come she walked to the edge of the cliff?"

"So, what's wrong with that?" "You worry too much. No one is going to suspect anything. Now, sit down in the rocker and we'll be here when he wakes up."

"Oh! I forgot that he asked me why we changed the pumpkin beds."

"Oh, really!" Alice said in surprise.

Agnes stopped thinking about the earlier events when she could hear Dickie and Alice returning. She picked up the teapot to pour them more tea.

Maude and Dickie drank their tea and Dickie asked them why they didn't drink the tea.

"Because, we'd be going to the bathroom all night! When you get our age you have to stop drinking at six o'clock or you're up all night going to the bathroom."

Maude sat her cup down and told everyone that she was going to take a luxurious bath. "I've been eyeing that tub since we got here and I hear it calling me, so I'm going to go and have a bubble bath."

"I think that I'll just stay here and watch the pumpkins," Dickie said as he sipped more special herbal tea.

Alice and Agnes giggled as Agnes told Maude that she'd bring her another cup of tea after she soaked in the tub.

Maude got up and walked in the house. Dickie sipped his tea and stared at the pumpkin beds. He asked, "Which one of you watches those VHS tapes of Cheech and Chong?"

Agnes smiled and looked at Alice. "We both do. We love Cheech and Chong and we need a laugh every now and then so we pop one in and watch it."

"You just don't seem the type to be watching Cheech and Chong."

Alice smiled and laughed her crazy laugh. "What type do we seem to be to you?"

"Oh, I don't know." Dickie was afraid to answer because he didn't want to offend them. "I think that you're very nice and I wouldn't mind having you for an aunt."

Alice laughed again and smiled at Agnes. "I don't know about you, but I think that I will get ready for bed." Agnes sat in her chair rocking, staring at the floor.

Alice said a bit louder, "I said, I think that I'll go up and get ready for bed. It's been a long day for us."

Agnes looked up at Alice. "Oh!..Yeah!...Me too!"

"Dickie, I hope you don't mind if we turn in and leave you sitting here all by yourself."

"Oh, no, not at all! I'll just stay here and drink my tea." Alice and Agnes smiled and walked in the house, leaving Dickie alone with his thoughts.

Dickie turned to look and make sure that they had gone in the house. He sat in his rocker until they turned off all the floodlights. He sneaked out into the pumpkin field to watch for their bedroom light to go out. He then quietly walked over to the special pumpkin beds.

Alice and Agnes peered out the window from above watching Dickie's every move. He walked around the patch and spotted a small pumpkin.

"I need to take the cup of special tea to Maude and I'll be right back," Agnes said as she quietly walked out the door.

Alice continued to watch Dickie as he bent down to touch one of their little baby pumpkins. "I wonder if they would miss this little guy?"

Agnes knocked on the door of the bathroom as Maude soaked in the bubble bath. "Come in."

Agnes entered carrying a cup of tea and sat it down on the rim of the bathtub. "You look like you're enjoying yourself."

"Oh, yes! This bath is wonderful and that cup of tea will be the finishing touch," Maude said as she reached for the tea. "I don't know what you put in this tea but it makes me so relaxed."

Agnes stood there and smiled as Maude took another sip.

"You have to tell me what you put in this tea," Maude said as she took another big sip and then sat the cup down on the rim of the tub.

"That's our secret, too!"

Maude could feel that she was getting very giddy and she replied,

"Everything is a secret."

"Yes! That's how we've stayed in here so long."

"Well, I guess that I'll just enjoy it while I'm here."

"Yes! Enjoy it while you're here…because tomorrow you won't be here."

"Oh, yes, we have to leave," Maude said as she took another sip of her tea and then leaned back in the bubble bath. "I must go now. If you need anything, just yell for me." Agnes smiled as she walked to the door.

"This is wonderful." Maude took another sip of her tea. Agnes turned to look at her. "Yes, it is, isn't it?"

Agnes laughed and walked out the door and closed it behind her, stopping to pick up the cell phone on her way out the bedroom door.

Maude stared at the door for a minute and thought, "They're always laughing. Oh, well! I guess I would too if all I ever did was talk to pumpkins."

When Maude finished drinking the whole cup of tea, she sat the cup down on the rim, leaned back, closed her eyes and fell asleep fast.

Meanwhile, Dickie had picked the small pumpkin and held it up to look at it in the moonlight. As he did this, George let out a big screech. Dickie turned to look at him and saw that all the pumpkins had great big eyes and mouths; he was afraid to move. The pumpkins began to chant. It sounded like they were saying, "Run, run, run!" Dickie looked at George again and was petrified. "I must be dreaming," he said.

Alice watched Dickie from their window. Agnes walked in the bedroom very quietly and walked over to stand behind Alice.

"Did he pick the pumpkin that we fixed for him?"

"Yes, but Kitty is ready to attack him."

Just then a loud bang was heard downstairs and Kitty ran away. Dickie took the pumpkin and ran and hid behind the pumpkin people.

"What was that?" Alice said as they headed for the door and ran down the stairs to the pumpkin patch.

The door to Maude's bathroom slowly opened and a figure dressed all in black tiptoed into the room and stood over her, looking at the empty teacup sitting on the rim and smiling. The intruder then took Maude's head and slowly pushed her lifeless body down into the bubble bath and held her there for a few minutes. The intruder dried a hand on the towel, and looked at Maude and whispered, "Good riddance!" The intruder then hurriedly left the room.

Downstairs, Alice and Agnes ran out into the pumpkin patch to search for Dickie.

"Dickie, where are you? We saw you take the pumpkin!"

Agnes ran back to the porch and climbed the steps; she turned around to see if she could see Dickie. He tried to hide behind one of the pumpkin people but they grabbed him instead.

"Come on, Dickie. Give me the pumpkin back," Alice said as she stood in front of him.

Dickie held on to the baby pumpkin as the pumpkin people held him.

"No!...No!...I have to be the master pastry chef...I desperately need this pumpkin."

Alice demanded that Dickie give him the pumpkin back.

"No!"

Alice motioned for the pumpkin people. "Open the pumpkin bed."

"Don't try to scare me," Dickie said as he clung to the pumpkin.

Alice stood in the path in front of him, "Oh, don't worry, I'm not trying to scare you."

"Then let me keep the pumpkin."

"No!...No!...No!...." Alice said as she walked around to grab the pumpkin out of Dickie's hand. The pumpkin bed began to open.

Dickie ran around the pumpkin bed as all the pumpkins began to chant, "Run,run,run!"

"Please, let me keep the pumpkin."

The pumpkins began to chant again, "No,no,no!"

Dickie pleaded with Alice. "I'll share my fortune with you."

"We don't need your fortune."

Agnes chimed in; " No! We don't need your fortune."

"Then, why can't I have just one of your pumpkins?"

"Because you won't have any use for it," Alice said smiling.

Dickie ran around the pumpkin bed as Alice chased him.

"This one little pumpkin can make me rich and famous."

"Where you're going, you won't need any money," Alice said very defiantly.

Dickie stopped running and stared at her; Agnes sneaked up behind him.

"What do you mean, I won't need any money?"

Agnes grabbed for the pumpkin and Dickie lost his balance trying to hang on to it. Alice tripped him and he fell backward into the pumpkin bed; he hit his head on the bottom of the bed.

Agnes held onto the baby pumpkin as they stood and looked at Dickie. "Boys!..Quick!.. Close the pumpkin bed." The pumpkin man pushed the lever and the pumpkin bed closed. Agnes put the baby pumpkin back on top of the bed. She brushed off her apron and said, "Well! I guess that's that."

Alice stood there smiling. "He was the sweetest one yet."

"Yes, he was!" Agnes added as they headed up the path toward the porch.

"I think that I had better go check on Maude," Agnes said as she stepped onto the veranda.

"I'll sit here and watch the pumpkin bed and make sure that he doesn't get out," Alice said as she sat down on one of the rockers.

Agnes stood in the hallway listening for any sounds that might come out of the bathroom.

Agnes knocked on the door and when no one answered, she called out, "Maude? Maude, are you in there?"

When Maude didn't answer, Agnes opened the door very slowly and peered in. She didn't see Maude sitting in the tub where she had left her.

"Oh, my gosh! She isn't in here!" Agnes walked back into the bedroom and suddenly said, "Henry must have taken her. That's probably what that noise was."

Agnes looked at her watch and said, "That's right, Henry was coming over at nine o'clock."

15

The next day the Bargain Basement truck stopped in the driveway. Alice and Agnes walked out to the front porch to make sure that he took everything.

The driver said, "We sure appreciate all the good clothes and stuff that you give us."

"Oh, we're just helping out our friends," Alice said smiling.

"I just don't understand how people can give away such good stuff, especially their good luggage. This stuff looks brand new."

The driver put Maude and Dickie's new luggage in the truck and got their receipt out of the cab.

Agnes stuck her hand out to take the receipt and said, "We need the writeoffs."

"Seniors' shouldn't have to pay taxes," the driver said as he climbed in the truck. He waved good-bye and headed out toward the gate.

Agnes waved and said, "Bye! Bye!"

Alice was a little perturbed. "Seniors! If I was a witch, I'd put a hex on him."

Agnes smiled and said, "Maybe, I should give him some tea."

"No tea for him. He's one that we would have to throw over the cliff."

Agnes frowned and said, "What would Henry do with that truck?"

"I see a taxi coming, maybe that's Henry," Alice said as she stood waiting for the taxi to arrive.

Henry got out and walked up to Alice and Agnes.

Alice was so excited to show him his new car. "Look what we've got for you."

Alice pointed to Dickies' shiny new red convertible.

"Ahhhhh! Cousin Alice, I wanted a shiny squad car!"

"Listen, Henry!" Agnes began but Alice patted her on the shoulder and walked up to Henry.

"Henry! We can't give you a shiny squad car or we'll all be in trouble."

Henry scuffed his feet on the pavement. Alice took the keys out of her apron pocket and handed them to Henry. He looked at the keys.

"This is something new. I've never seen a key ring with a chef's hat on it," Henry said as he got in the car and looked at the gearshift.

"Look how beautiful the car is, Henry," Alice said.

Agnes wanted to make him feel better. "Henry, you look fabulous in your new little red sports car."

"Yeah, but it doesn't have all the bells and whistles."

Agnes was getting frustrated with Henry. "The only thing that I know that has a bell and whistle is a fire truck and you know that we can't get you one of those."

"Why not?" Henry started the car and drove off down the road toward the gate.

"Kids! You can never please them," Alice said as she turned to go in the house.

"He said he wanted a shiny red car," Agnes added.

Later that afternoon, Agnes sat in her chair gazing at the ocean when she heard a knock at the front door and went to answer it.

She opened the door to see a young woman standing there smiling at her.

Agnes smiled back and said, "Hello! Can I help you?"

The young woman answered her by saying. "Hello, my name is Kitty. Can I come in?"

"Oh, yes. I like kitties," Agnes said as she opened the door for the woman to come in.

Agnes told Kitty to sit down in one of the rockers on the veranda. She took out her new cell phone from Maude and called Alice. Kitty looked at Agnes' cell phone and smiled.

"We have company."

Agnes closed the cell phone and put it back in her pocket.

Kitty smiled and said, "Your pumpkin beds look fabulous."

"Would you like some tea?"

"Sure! But, first, can you tell me how you can get your pumpkins to glow like they do?"

Agnes looked at the pumpkin beds and smiled, "Well, that's a big secret."

"Oh, really?"

Agnes was getting nervous without Alice so she said, "Why don't I go get our tea and then we can talk."

Agnes went inside and Kitty sat in the rocker, rocking and smiling.

Agnes came back in a few minutes with a tray that had two cups on it and a pot of tea. One cup had already been filled.

Agnes sat the tray down, filled a cup of tea and handed it to Kitty. She then walked to the door and yelled for Alice. Agnes heard Alice yell for her and went inside. After Agnes walked inside the house, Kitty switched the teacups, leaned back in her chair and smiled.

Agnes walked back out to the porch and sat down. She smiled at Kitty as she took a sip of her tea.

As the sun began to fade Kitty asked, "Isn't this a wonderful time of the day?"

Agnes tried to speak but the words wouldn't come out so she drank the rest of her tea; she then sat the cup down.

Kitty looked at Agnes and asked, "Are you all right?"

"I…think…so!"

Kitty continued to rock in her chair until Agnes slumped over.

"Ummmmmmmmm!"

Kitty got up and walked over to Agnes and said, "Maybe, we had better go for a walk."

Agnes slowly said, "O…k…a...y."

Kitty helped Agnes get up and slowly walk down the steps to the front of the pumpkin bed. She smiled at the pumpkin people and motioned to them to open the bed.

Agnes saw the bed opening and could barely get the words out, "What's going on?"

Kitty smiled as she said, "You need to take a long nap."

"No!...No, I don't!" She reached for her cell phone.

"Yes, you do! But, first, give me back my cell phone."

"Cell phone? No!.. You can't have my cell phone." Agnes cried.

"It's not your cell phone. It's mine!"

Agnes looked at Kitty. She didn't understand. Kitty grabbed the cell phone from Agnes' hand, pushed Agnes onto the open bed and motioned for the pumpkin people to close the bed.

As the bed closed, she yelled at Agnes, "Oh! By the way, I hated my sister. She had everything, a wonderful marriage, a brand-new house, a great job and I had nothing. Now I've got it all.

Kitty turned to walk back to the house when Alice appeared. "Where's Agnes and who are you?"

"Agnes is in a nice comfortable place with some really nice people."

"What do you mean?"

Kitty smiled and said, "Agnes finished making the bed!" Alice gasped and grabbed her stomach and stared at Kitty.

"It's like you've always said; only the best will do!"

"What are you talking about?" Alice said as she backed away from Kitty.

"Don't play innocent with me. You've had your fun all these years. Now it's my turn," Kitty said.

She motioned for the pumpkin people to help her. "Boys!"

Alice couldn't believe her eyes and yelled at the pumpkin people. "Boys!"

Kitty began to chant with the pumpkins, "Run! Run! Run!"

The pumpkin people begin to form a circle around Alice. She broke through and ran as fast as she could and they began to run after her. She had run in the wrong direction and now was standing at the edge of the cliff,

"Help! Help!"

"Cry all you want, cause no one is going to hear you."

"I don't understand," Alice cried just as Henry walked up.

"Henry! Thank God you're here. You've got to save me."

Henry smiled at Alice and said, "You're making too much noise."

Alice pleaded with Henry to help her. "Please, Henry, please help me."

Henry walked over to Cousin Alice and pushed her over the cliff.

Alice screamed all the way down to the bottom.

"H…E…N…R…Y!"

The next afternoon, Kitty and Henry sat on the veranda eating their pumpkin bread and drinking the regular herbal tea and rocked in their rocking chairs.

Henry looked at Kitty and said, "Now, can I have my squad car?"

Kitty sat her cup of tea down and reached in her pocket, pulled out her cell phone and opened it, punched in a number and waited.

"Sergeant? This is Kitty. I'm staying at The Pumpkin Patch Bed and Breakfast and I'm afraid that there has been a terrible accident."

Henry smiled.

"Yes…yes…that will be fine," Kitty said as she smiled and closed the cell phone.

Henry waited for her to respond and finally said, "And?"

Kitty looked at Henry and said with a big smile, "He'll be here in a few minutes."